MURDER IN THE WOLF PEN

Thor and the other wolf had gotten into some kind of tussle over a bone, yipping and snarling. Rich signaled that it was time to leave, so I turned off the water and gave Freya one last pat. She slunk off toward her favored rocky outcropping, and the fighting wolves stopped for a moment to watch her. I zipped ahead of Rich, and we were out of the gate in seconds.

As Thor and his frisky friend trotted closer to Freya, I hesitated. "Is she going to be okay?"

Rich chuckled. "Oh, sure. That's a mild fight—they scrap around nearly every day. Freya can hold her own, trust me."

I felt more confident as we made our way to the second enclosure. Rich instructed me to fill the watering trough again, and I appreciated the way he was letting me ease into my role.

The double gates came into view. Since I was in front, I slowed for Rich to wheel his way closer.

I glanced at the enclosure, trying to locate the trough. But my gaze settled on something else—something that was utterly disturbing.

Just inside the second gate, it was plain to see that Njord, the white pack leader, had red stains all over his beautiful coat. He was standing sentry over something—no, *someone.*

Someone in a neon-green vest.

Books by Heather Day Gilbert

BELINDA BLAKE AND THE SNAKE IN THE GRASS

BELINDA BLAKE AND THE WOLF IN SHEEP'S CLOTHING

Published by Kensington Publishing Corporation

Belinda Blake and the Wolf in Sheep's Clothing

Heather Day Gilbert

LYRICAL UNDERGROUND
Kensington Publishing Corp.
www.kensingtonbooks.com

LYRICAL UNDERGROUND BOOKS are published by

Kensington Publishing Corp.
119 West 40th Street
New York, NY 10018

All Kensington titles, imprints, and distributed lines are available at special quantity discounts for bulk purchases for sales promotion, premiums, fund-raising, educational, or institutional use.

Special book excerpts or customized printings can also be created to fit specific needs. For details, write or phone the office of the Kensington Sales Manager: Kensington Publishing Corp., 119 West 40th Street, New York, NY 10018. Attn. Sales Department. Phone: 1-800-221-2647.

Lyrical Underground and Lyrical Underground logo Reg. US Pat. & TM Off.

First Electronic Edition: October 2019
ISBN-13: 978-1-5161-0882-4 (ebook)
ISBN-10: 1-5161-0882-5 (ebook)

First Print Edition: October 2019
ISBN-13: 978-1-5161-0885-5
ISBN-10: 1-5161-0885-X

Printed in the United States of America

1

Rainy weather was an introvert's best friend.

At least that's the way I'd felt for years, but after four days of nonstop drizzle alternating with heavy deluges in Greenwich, Connecticut, I was about to change my mind. I needed to get out of my stone carriage house, needed to take in the rich smells of spring, needed to touch the velvety red tulip petals that had finally started to unfurl in my flower bed out back.

I cozied up on my blue couch, setting my warm mug of Arabica coffee on the low table in front of me. Snagging one of my favorite Agatha Christie mysteries, *By the Pricking of My Thumbs*, off my shelf, I tried to pick up where I'd left off.

Instead, my gaze wandered to my wide front window, where I could see the shamrock-green lawn stretching up to the Carringtons' manor house. I tried not to think of my last encounter with Stone Carrington the fifth, but I couldn't help myself.

When Stone had broken a couple months' silence and shown up on my doorstep in early March, it was obvious something had changed. I could see it in his face—the way those turquoise eyes shone with expectation. I figured he'd tell me he'd found someone who'd made him forget all the stresses of his complicated family life.

Instead, he'd said something far worse.

He was heading to Bhutan.

Dietrich, our artist friend, had told Stone about a yoga retreat in the mountains of Bhutan that had revolutionized his perspective on just about everything. After researching the retreat, Stone had decided it might be just the thing to clear his head.

"I have to get strong enough to fight my own demons," he'd said.

"I think you already are," I'd responded.

He had smiled wistfully, then pulled me into a hug. His luxuriant leathery scent utterly wrecked my ability to concentrate, so I relaxed into his long arms.

"I'm glad you believe in me, Belinda." His lips had brushed my curls as he murmured into my hair. "And Dad's partner assures me that it's all systems go for me to take over the family hedge fund business. But I don't feel right stepping into that position until I'm sure that's what I want to do. I don't want to be locked into a life that sucks out my soul." He drew back, and I met his serious gaze. "You understand what I mean. Look at you—you started a pet-sitting business in Manhattan, then you moved to Greenwich and grew your clientele even more. I love that you're so unafraid. That's how I want to live."

Several responses had run through my mind, but I was only able to articulate one.

"I do understand," I'd said.

And with that, I'd inadvertently given my blessing on Stone's big adventure, but I knew that was the way it should be. I would never hold someone back from finding their purpose in life.

Besides, my feelings for Stone were seriously conflicted. Since my visit home at Christmas, my parents' neighbor, dairy farmer Jonas Hawthorne, had given me weekly calls to discuss the classics I was reading along with his book club. Every time I hung up the phone with him, I found myself smiling like I'd won the sweepstakes. I hadn't analyzed our relationship yet, but I was pretty sure my psychologist sister, Katrina, would be more than happy to help me figure things out.

Life in the carriage house had seemed dreadfully boring since Stone hopped his plane for Bhutan. Doubtless, he'd had a full month of epiphanies while I'd stayed mostly housebound, playing video games and taking every pet-sitting job I could to pay the bills.

I turned back to *By the Pricking of My Thumbs*. I was reading the same sentence for the fourth time when my cell phone rang. I grabbed it from the coffee table and barked, "Hello," without even bothering to check who was calling first.

A woman's soft voice filled the line. "Is this Belinda Blake, the pet-sitter?"

"It is." I was ready to jump on any sitting job she offered, because it'd been two weeks since my last one.

"I'm Dahlia White. I have several large-breed animals I was wondering if you'd be available to help care for. You'd need to start in a couple of days, and I'd need you for an eight-day stint. I'm sorry it's such late notice, but the other person I asked wasn't able to do it."

Dogs—my favorite. I responded enthusiastically. "Sure thing. I grew up with German shepherds, so I'm no stranger to the larger breeds."

After a miniscule pause, Dahlia responded. "Well, that's the thing. They're not dogs—they're wolves."

I caught my breath as she rushed on.

"But my fluffy darlings are no trouble to care for, I promise. They're like my babies. You wouldn't have to do much, just help my primary feeder with his chores so he wouldn't have to stay overtime to get things done. Since you'd advertised that you specialize in exotic pets, I assumed you would be quite comfortable with unusual jobs like this."

I hesitated. I'd never been to a wolf preserve—much less seen a wolf up close—but the way Dahlia was talking, you'd think they were just like dogs.

"Um." I floundered about for something to say, but nothing coherent sprang to mind.

"I'll tell you what, why don't you look up the preserve website online and check us out? It's the White Pine Wolf Preserve site. Many of our guests have left reviews of their tour experience, and they're all extremely positive about their interactions with the wolves."

"Okay. I'll do that and get back to you." I wanted to buy myself time.

"That sounds great. Actually, if it's not too much trouble, could you call me back in a couple of hours so I'll know if I need to find someone else?" She gave a brief pause. "Oh, and I forgot to mention that I'll pay top dollar for your services—I know you come highly qualified."

She must have read my endorsements from the Greenwich and Manhattan elite. I always tried to snag a quote when one of my wealthy clients praised my pet-sitting skills.

I had to admit, the top-dollar payment Dahlia promised was more than a little tempting because it was sorely needed. I agreed to check out the preserve and touch base in an hour. As I hung up the phone, a book slid from my overstuffed bookshelf and hit the floor.

I walked over to pick it up and glanced at the title.

White Fang.

Was it a good sign, a bad sign, or just a coincidence?

At this point, it was impossible to guess.

* * * *

The White Pine Wolf Preserve website yielded minimal information. As I should have guessed, the featured reviews were completely positive. One guest bragged about how her autistic son had made an instant connection with a white wolf and had enjoyed his time petting it. A teen posted that during the tour, a timber wolf had begged for his piece of watermelon—and when he'd offered it through the fence, the wolf had gobbled it up and begged for more.

I clicked on Dahlia White's "About the Owner" section, and it certainly tugged at the heartstrings. Dahlia had rescued her animals from lives of fighting or even from euthanization.

"Once I knew of the plight of these animals, it would have been heartless to walk away," Dahlia was quoted as saying in the local paper. "My animals have found healing here, and it's a joy to share their stories with our visitors."

Everything sounded very professional, and the pictures showed people and wolves frolicking like it was the most normal thing in the world. The grounds looked spotless, and the wolves had clean teeth and coats, so it seemed they were well looked after.

I grabbed an umbrella, unable to sit around any longer. After pulling on my rubber boots, I sloshed out to the mailbox. My mom had mentioned that she'd sent me a care package, and I'd been anxiously awaiting it, even though I knew it would likely be filled with inedible cookies, healthy snacks, and vitamins the size of horse pills.

Creaking open the black mailbox door, I peered inside. There didn't seem to be a yellow package slip. Instead, I withdrew a handful of bills. I didn't even want to think about whether I had the money in my account to cover these, plus the rent, plus repairs on my car.

My older-model Volvo, which I fondly referred to as Bluebell, was temporarily out of commission. Bluebell had decided to shed her rusting tailpipe smack in the middle of I-95, and I was still waiting for the replacement to come in.

Sure, I could ask my parents for money, but it felt like giving up to have to do that. I had survived in Manhattan, scraping by on smaller pet-sitting jobs, so when I moved to Greenwich last year, I'd had high hopes that my business would take off.

Although Greenwich had widened my clientele, my income was still somewhat sporadic. And, truth be told, I needed an influx of money right now. My video game review checks wouldn't arrive until the end of April.

I shoved the mail into my jeans pocket and trudged back to my house. I knew what I had to do. Besides, it couldn't be that hard to work at a wolf preserve, could it? And the experience would look fantastic in the bio on my website. I mean, if I could handle pet-sitting wolves, what *couldn't* I handle?

Summoning my confidence, I dialed Dahlia's number and agreed to come in the next morning to sign the contract and tour the facility. She sounded understandably relieved. The number of people in Greenwich who would like to work with wolves could probably be counted on one hand—and I was betting those were the people who were already employed at the preserve.

Once I'd squared things away with Dahlia, my next call was to Red, the Carringtons' chauffeur. Once Stone the fourth had heard my car was in the shop, he'd volunteered Red's driving services so I could get where I needed to go. I wasn't sure if Stone the elder was being kind because I was a good tenant or because he felt he owed me something since I'd narrowly escaped a life-or-death situation in his house this past winter.

Red's gruff voice filled the line. "Yes?"

Red's ex-army persona didn't throw me, even though his habit of carrying concealed weapons did make him seem more like a bodyguard than a proper chauffeur.

"Red, could you run me somewhere tomorrow morning? We can stop for Dunkin' Donuts." I knew Red had a sweet spot for their oversized bear claw pastries.

"You don't have to butter me up, Belinda." He chuckled. "I'll take you wherever you need to go. What time?"

"How about eight-thirty—that'll give us a little time to stop by Dunkin' D. And no, I'm not buttering you up—I promise. I like their coffee."

However, if the coffee and bear claw happened to loosen Red's lips as to any updates about Stone the fifth, it would be a happy bonus.

* * * *

Red pulled up ten minutes early, but I'd known this was his habit, so I was ready. I had donned jeans, my Doc Martens, and a light blue, paint-splattered Columbia University hoodie I'd swiped from my dad the last time I visited home. Normally, I wouldn't wear such casual gear for my first visit with a client, but the wolves were outside, and though the rain had stopped, the ground had turned to mush.

I splashed through a couple of puddles to meet Red, who had walked around to open the door for me. He didn't bat an eye at my unusual attire, but instead tipped his chauffeur's hat toward me in an old-fashioned gesture of respect that warmed my heart. Red always made me feel like I fit into Greenwich society, even though it was quite obvious I didn't.

Sharing Dahlia's address, I carefully omitted the fact that we were heading to a wolf preserve. If Red knew what I was stepping into, it was possible he'd balk at driving me there, and I didn't want to have to pay for a cab or car service.

On the way, Red stopped at the Dunkin' Donuts drive-through to pick up our goodies. He drove into a parking spot and distributed our food.

I took a slow sip of the deliciously strong coffee. Red pulled the tab back on his cup and positioned it in the holder, then started backing the car out.

I tried to sound casual. "So, has Stone called lately from Bhutan?"

The middle-aged chauffeur threw a quick glance at me in the rearview mirror. "Matter of fact, he did call, just yesterday. Wanted me to take his car in for inspection—he remembered it expires this month." His lips curled into a half smile as he bit into his bear claw, bits of icing dropping all over the napkin in his lap.

I wasn't sure if he was smiling about the pastry, or about having the opportunity to get behind the wheel of Stone's yellow Lamborghini. I figured it was the Lamborghini.

An inadvertent sigh escaped my lips, which seemed to trigger Red's memory.

"He did ask about you," he added hastily.

"And?"

Red grinned. "He wondered if you'd been pet-sitting any more snakes."

I'd watched a ball python named Rasputin last year, and the experience was memorable, to say the least. "Ha. No more snakes of late."

I didn't add that I'd made a few trips into Manhattan just to see Rasputin. I kind of owed that snake, after all, and on some reptilian level, I was convinced he liked me.

Chartreuse-budded tree limbs arced alongside the road as we drove through a heavily wooded area. When Red slowed to turn off on Dahlia's road, I realized we'd gone a full three minutes without seeing one typical Greenwich McMansion—or any houses at all. Although I'd grown up in a rural area, the complete seclusion of Dahlia's wolf preserve felt a little sinister.

Halfway up the drive, a gate stood open, with a large sign affixed to it reading *White Pine Wolf Preserve*. My cover was blown. I slid down lower in the seat because I knew what was coming next.

Red pulled to an abrupt stop and turned to stare at me. "You sure this is the right place?"

I didn't meet his eyes. "Yes, it is. This is the address I gave you, right?"

He didn't even bother to answer my question. "Will you be working directly with wolves? This job sounds too risky."

"I don't know the details yet," I answered honestly. "And the owner said they're perfectly safe."

"Of course she would," Red muttered into his coffee cup.

2

"Please keep driving," I said firmly.

Red finally gave a half-hearted nod and gently pressed the gas. As we neared the end of the long, paved drive, the White Pine Wolf Preserve began to resemble the tourist destination it was. An extended, renovated red barn bore a *Visitors' Center* sign. Behind the barn, I caught a glimpse of a white farmhouse with fresh new siding. Red pulled into a space in the good-sized parking lot adjacent to the barn.

He seemed to struggle for words, like he was hoping I'd back out of this, but his chauffeur decorum won out. "What time should I pick you up?" he asked briskly.

"I'll text you." I couldn't allow myself to chicken out, uneasy as I felt. Dahlia was counting on me, and I knew she'd never find anyone else on such short notice.

Since no one had appeared to greet me, I gave a brief, hopefully confident nod to Red and stepped out of the car. I shouldered my purse and strode toward the barn. The outside bore a glossy coat of apple-red paint, and plum and lemon colored pansies had been painstakingly planted in the window boxes.

I pushed open the rustic wooden door. The inside of the visitors' center was just as carefully kept. The walnut plank floors and massive overhead beams emphasized the spaciousness of the barn. The shop was well organized, and I didn't find myself bumping into display tables like I usually did in places like this. Although there were the predictable wolf trinkets and T-shirts, it was the homemade items such as natural stone jewelry, handmade soaps, and unusual jellies that drew my eye. Burning wax melts and small twinkle-light grapevine trees lent the place a welcoming air.

"Good morning." A chic woman with a British accent stepped from behind the natural wood counter and made her way toward me. "How may I help you today? Were you interested in a tour?"

"Actually, I was looking for the owner, Dahlia White. I'm supposed to be helping with her animals."

The woman smiled, adjusting the silk scarf knotted around her slim neck. With her dark pixie haircut and flawless makeup, she looked like she belonged in an upscale art gallery, not working the cash register at a wolf preserve.

"You must be Belinda!" she said, extending a hand. "Dahlia had to motor into town before her trip, so I was instructed to have Shaun give you a tour around our facilities. I'm Evie Grady, by the way—Dahlia's administrative assistant."

Evie pulled a cell phone from her pocket, punching in a number to call Shaun, whoever he was. After a brief conversation, she returned her attention to me.

"He'll be here in a moment. Shaun Fowler has worked at White Pine since it opened three years ago, and he's one of the best tour guides out there. He puts the tourists at ease with his sense of humor, which is important for their first encounter with the wolves."

I still found it hard to believe I was gearing up for *my* first wolf encounter. "That's wonderful," I murmured.

Oblivious to my discomfort, Evie launched into a brief tour of the visitors' center, which boasted a kitchen area where employees could get coffee and take lunch breaks. She also pointed out a hand-drawn, framed map of the preserve that hung over the mantel of the stone fireplace.

"We have a thirty-acre fenced area for the packs," she said, gesturing to a thick green border line on the map.

There was more than one pack?

Evie rolled on with her monologue. "Shaun will be able to tell you more about each of the animals and how they came to us. I'm sure it won't take you long to acclimate to the routine, given that you specialize in exotic pets?"

"I should be able to pick things up quickly," I said. "I'm good with animals."

And not just any animals. The truth was that I'd built my business by watching the animals other sitters didn't want to touch. The wealthy tended to buy unusual pets, and they didn't like to leave them unattended when they went on trips. It was usually a win-win for me when the pets were easy to care for, like hermit crabs or turtles. Wolves had never factored into my consideration before, but I reassured myself that I would be well-compensated for whatever I was required to do on the preserve.

An oversized fellow bumbled into the door. He wore a neon-green vest that had the preserve name emblazoned on it in white reflective lettering.

"Hi, I'm Shaun," he said, giving me a relaxed smile. "I take it you're Belinda Blake?" His eyes traveled over my hair, then slowed as they reached my face. His freckled cheeks flushed. "Say, you wouldn't happen to be the Belinda Blake who's a game reviewer, would you? You kind of look like her."

I was surprised, but flattered. I beamed at him. "I'm that Belinda, yes."

His eyes widened. "I read your reviews every month. You're one of the best."

"Thanks," I said. I couldn't help warming to a kindred gamer spirit.

I'd been reviewing video games in my free time for years, but since I'd landed a regular column at a bigger magazine early last year, I'd picked up substantially more followers. In fact, I was about to launch my own Twitch stream, where gamers could watch me live-play some of the newest releases.

"Let me get you a vest," he said, rushing into the kitchen and retrieving one. As he handed it over, I pretended to shield my eyes from the green glare.

"It's quite loud, but it keeps the employees visible," he explained, then gestured toward my right pocket. "There's a pepper spray in every vest, just in case of emergencies."

I patted at the canister in my pocket and raised my eyebrows.

"It's standard at wild animal preserves like this," he said. "Trust me, I've never used mine."

Shaun headed outside, so I followed him. It was a good thing I'd worn a hoodie, because the fickle April temperature had dropped since morning.

Shaun led me up a wide trail into the woods. A tall, chain-link fence came into view.

"It's eight feet high, just to be on the safe side," he explained. "We have to pay close attention after storms, because if a tree falls on the fence, those wolves can climb right up and out. They're very resourceful." He sounded like a doting father, proud of his child for doing something like punching the class bully.

"How'd you get interested in wolves?" I asked, my Doc Martens sinking into yet another puddle.

"I met Dahlia when she toured the nature center I used to work at in Stamford. She told me she was going to open a wolf preserve in Greenwich, and she said she was looking for outstanding tour guides, like me. I started working here the first day White Pine opened—about four months after we'd met."

I wanted to know more about my new employer. "So Dahlia already had experience with wolves?"

Shaun ground a sprouting blackberry vine underfoot. "Nope. Not a bit, actually. She was coming off a divorce, and she wanted to use this property in hopes of making a difference in the world. After reading up on wolf and wolf-dog breeding, she discovered that many of those animals wind up abandoned or euthanized because they're so uncontrollable—not surprising, because they're wild, right? Anyway, she dedicated herself to providing a shelter for them."

"That's admirable," I said, nearly running into Shaun's wide back as he paused to toss a rock from the path.

"Yeah, and Dahlia's also the one who puts in long hours to make sure each new wolf is integrated into a pack. We have two packs here, and at the moment, each pack has three wolves. Creating packs isn't easy—it can be brutal, like *The Hunger Games*. See, in the wild, packs form naturally around animals from the same bloodline. But in captivity, wolves can resort to serious infighting to establish dominance. I hate to say it, but omega wolves sometimes get killed in the process."

I slowed. So I'd signed up for an eight-day job, working with beasts who even killed their own kind? Maybe I should get out now, while the getting was good.

Shaun hiked past a double-gated entrance set into the fence line. A slight movement caught my eye, and I peered into the enclosed area. A gangly brown wolf with a black face was perched on a rock, her eyes fixed on me. It was quite mesmerizing. I actually started walking toward the fence, but Shaun didn't notice and kept plowing forward on the trail. I hurried to catch up and realized he was asking questions about my latest game review.

He finally stopped when we came to a second gated enclosure. After opening the first set of gates, Shaun led me toward the second. A large white wolf loped our way, shoving its nose through the chain links. Shaun gave the animal's nose and part of its muzzle a thorough petting, and I could swear the wolf was smiling.

The wolf turned its butterscotch colored eyes to me. I wasn't sure how to mask my fear, but I knew enough not to stare right into its eyes. The wolf sniffed at the air, and I took a brief glance at its face.

It appeared that the animal was merely curious, not hostile.

"This one's named Njord," Shaun explained. "He's the only wolf that's been bred in captivity on the preserve, and he's the alpha of this pack."

He reached out, and the wolf approached his hand again. "And as you can see, he's about as tame as a wolf can be. He's my favorite to take into the crowd when I give a tour."

Njord licked his lips, and the sudden sharpness in his look made me antsy. "Is he hungry?" I asked.

"Might be. That's not my job—Rich O'Brien handles that end of things. We'll catch up with him today so he can show you what's what."

Leaving Njord lingering at the fence line, we headed out of the enclosure and back onto the trail. Shadowy forest branches filtered the sunlight, and we walked alongside a full, rippling creek that probably supplied water to the wolves. If Shaun wasn't with me, I'd be tempted to grab a book and a blanket and plop down on one of the rocky overhangs. The extensive grounds really seemed like the perfect place to be alone with nature and one's own thoughts.

A wolf's howl broke the silence, triggering a chorus of howling responses, but Shaun only grinned. "They talk to each other and sometimes to us. It tends to make the tourists nervous, but howling doesn't always mean wolves are on the prowl for food."

I was going to have to take his word for it, because to my ears, the howls sounded more than a little ominous.

The visitors' center eventually came into view, and I realized we'd made a complete loop around the property. A man emerged from the side door of the barn, loading something into a bucket in a wheelbarrow, and Shaun shouted to him. "Rich! I've got the new girl here."

Rich, a slim man in his mid-fifties, walked my way, but didn't extend a hand. "I have meat on my hands—loading it up for the wolves—but it's nice to meet you. Belinda, was it?"

"Yes, that's me. Belinda Blake."

Shaun gave me a quick grin. "It was great hanging with a gamer legend like yourself. Sorry if I geeked out a little. I'll catch you later."

My face colored a bit as Shaun lumbered off. Rich politely ignored my discomfiture and went back to raiding the off-white refrigerator in the kitchen. I made a mental note to store my lunch in the other fridge that had a sign marked *Staff Use*.

I held the side door open as Rich returned to deposit handfuls of raw meat into the bucket. Why didn't he bother wearing gloves for this messy operation?

"I like to use the wheelbarrow because it's less disruptive than the golf cart," Rich explained as he continued his back-and-forth. "And I don't touch the meat with gloves, so it smells more natural to the wolves."

I was impressed with the way Rich seemed to put the wolves first in his caretaking. It was the same way I tried to operate as a pet-sitter. We'd probably get along fine as I helped him...although it was beyond me how I would feed raw meat to wolves without looking like an oversized, tasty morsel myself.

Evie strolled into the kitchen. Her garnet lipstick had been freshly reapplied, and the faint smell of spicy perfume drifted our way. Rich seemed oblivious to Evie's high-class beauty, his final load of meats in hand as he used his backside to slam the fridge door shut.

Evie's nose wrinkled at the sight of the raw, red mess stuffed into the buckets, and she quickly turned to me. "Belinda, would you mind sticking close to the visitors' center? Maybe Rich can show you how to feed the wolves tomorrow. Dahlia's on her way back and she'll arrive soon, and I think you should talk with her to nail down details before she leaves on her trip."

"Sure." I certainly didn't mind postponing my first feeding adventure.

We took our leave of Rich and headed back into the gift shop. Evie's cell phone gave a metallic ring. When she picked up, her smile quickly faded and her tone turned serious. She strode out the main door, firmly closing it behind her.

Finding her secretive behavior strange, I absently started browsing the clothing racks. I was seriously contemplating picking up a snarling wolf T-shirt emblazoned with the words *Alpha Mom* for my pregnant sister, Katrina, when a hipster dude with clear plastic glasses walked in.

He breezed past me and entered the kitchen area. I realized he probably thought I was a tourist, so I followed him into the kitchen to introduce myself.

He had just settled into a chair and was aimlessly thumbing through his phone as if boredom was his personal cross to bear. He didn't even look up as I lurked in the doorway. When he continued to look at his phone, I cleared my throat.

After what felt like five minutes but was probably only one, he finally glanced up and grunted.

"You new here?" he asked.

I nodded, curious as to what his story was. "I'm Belinda. Do you work here, too?"

The guy offered a smile that didn't reach his eyes, revealing small, straight teeth. "I'm Carson White. My mom runs the place."

"Oh! Nice to meet you. I haven't met your mom yet."

As if he could care less, his eyes slid back to his phone screen. With his straight-leg blue chinos and plaid button-up shirt, he struck me as one of those preppy types who seemed endlessly restless and unhappy. As I turned to leave, a young woman with a long black ponytail walked in. Carson instantly snapped to attention the moment she spoke.

"Have you seen my vest?" she asked, but it sounded like a demand.

Carson jumped to his feet and began rummaging through the coatrack on the back wall. After he produced a lime-green vest and handed it to the woman, she turned to speak to me.

"You're the new girl, Belinda, right? I'm Veronica—I'm one of the tour guides."

Carson injected himself into our conversation, probably in an attempt to get Veronica to turn her luminous brown eyes his way. "She's working on her master's degree."

She shrugged her vest on over her fitted shirt. "I'm writing my thesis now. It's about the wolves, actually. I've titled it *Captive Wolves and Their Interactions with Humans: Pack or Prey?*"

The title seemed poorly worded to me, but it did seem like an interesting topic, and one Veronica would get plenty of fodder for while she worked at the preserve. I really hoped she'd conclude that captive wolves looked at humans like their pack, because the alternative was frightening.

Veronica swept out the side door, and Carson followed, hot on her heels. I was curious as to what Carson's relationship was with the lovely Veronica, if any. Had he been waiting here for her to show up?

I glanced out the window. Veronica was speed-walking toward the woods, leaving Carson in her dust. Apparently, the attraction wasn't mutual.

I headed back into the gift shop. Evie hadn't returned, and I wondered how long I was going to have to wait to meet Dahlia. I considered calling Red and asking him to pick me up, but instead I decided to take a little jaunt outside and try to get my bearings at my new job.

Just as I opened the front door, a green Prius whipped into a spot in front of the visitors' center and a woman seemed to wrestle with her seat before getting out. Her frowsy dishwater-blonde hair and worn chambray shirt, half-tucked into her jeans, gave the impression of someone who didn't put much time into her appearance—an anomaly in this town. Gripping a plastic shopping bag, she bustled to my side. Her eyes darted to my face, then to the woods, adding to the impression that she was a woman constantly in motion.

"Good to see you—Belinda, right? I'm Dahlia, the one who called you. I'm *so* sorry I wasn't here—I had to pick up some last-minute pet supplies, and the person ahead of me was buying out the store, it seemed!" She tried to shove her fluffy bangs to the side, but they curtained her eyes again. "Let's go inside, shall we? I need to talk with Evie briefly, then I'll explain your position to you."

"Actually, Evie's not in there right now," I said.

All her fidgeting stilled for a moment. "Really? That's not like her." She readjusted the bag in her hand, a bewildered look on her face. "Right. Well, let's go on in, and we'll talk about what you'll be doing here."

I pushed the door open so Dahlia could walk in first. I glanced around, then immediately felt like a liar. Evie was sitting at the kitchen table, munching on a half-eaten croissant.

Dahlia turned back to me with a strange expression, and I felt like I'd failed some kind of test. "She wasn't here when I walked outside," I rushed to explain.

"Of course," Dahlia said, but there was a dubious note in her voice.

As she bustled into the kitchen, I trailed behind, trying to understand why Evie had felt the need to come sneaking in the side door after her phone call. It seemed the administrative assistant was hiding something, and I wondered what it was.

3

As we drew closer, Evie wiped chocolate from her mouth and smiled. I felt a flash of jealousy. Of course she could eat fattening foods with no obvious side effects, unlike me. My mouth watered as I thought of my favorite sweet—my sister's fluffy cinnamon rolls. Every time we got together at our home in Larches Corner, New York, Katrina would bake nonstop, and I'd gain at least five pounds.

It was always worth it, though.

Evie must have shoved half of that croissant into her mouth the moment Dahlia had driven up, because she hadn't been in the kitchen when I walked out of the barn. I was pondering the reason for Evie's façade when Dahlia motioned for me to sit down.

"Belinda, again, I'm sorry to have to ask for your help on such short notice, but an unexpected opportunity came up," she began. "I've been corresponding with the owner of an Arizona wolf preserve for a year and a half, and he has some unusual ideas I'd like to integrate at White Pine. He recently asked if I'd like to do on-site observations, and I initially refused, but soon after that, I stumbled across a fantastic deal on flights. I decided to go for it at the last minute."

"Sounds like a good opportunity," I said, stealing a glance at Evie. She had already polished off the croissant and appeared to have drained an entire cup of coffee, as well.

Dahlia rubbed at her temples as if stressed. "I do hate to put you on the spot like this, but Rich's oldest daughter is getting married right after Easter, and he can't stay late for chores, since he's trying to refinish some of the floors in the older house she just bought. I just needed an extra pair of hands to lighten his load while I'm gone."

I nodded. Rich's attempt to refinish his daughter's floors sounded exactly like something my dad would try to do for me.

She continued, "Your jobs will include helping Rich feed the wolves—I suspect you'd just have to take care of their water supply, since Rich enjoys feeding the animals himself. Then we also have chickens, peacocks, and goats that will need to be fed."

She fell silent, and I realized she was waiting for some kind of response.

"Sure. Yes, I've fed goats and chickens before."

She gave a quick smile. "Good. It's hard to find people who are familiar with these kinds of chores. And as far as the wolves go, I knew you wouldn't be frightened since you're no stranger to out-of-the-ordinary pets."

I hoped she was right. What I'd seen of the wolves today hadn't been frightening—but I hadn't been inside their enclosures yet.

Dahlia brushed a crumb from the table. "Now, Evie will run the business end of things while I'm gone, and between her and Carson, I figure things will go smoothly. Even though Veronica is a natural with the wolves, I plan to keep her on tour guide duty so she can stay more impartial as she writes her thesis. As a guide, she can watch the way the wolves interact with both guests and caretakers."

"That makes sense," I said.

Dahlia turned to Evie. "Would you mind printing the contract?"

Evie stood and placed her mug in the sink. "I'd be happy to." She strode out.

Dahlia glanced at her watch. "I'll just go over it with you, but then I'd better get finished with my packing." She began to chatter on about the Arizona wolf preserve, but I only half-listened. After volunteering at my dad's veterinary clinic for years, I'd developed a talent for sifting animal conversations through the filter of what was actually relevant, and most of what Dahlia was telling me was inconsequential.

Evie returned and placed the contract and a black pen on the table. I started reading, feeling my eyebrows inching upward as I turned each page.

The contract was far from standard. It listed injuries I agreed not to hold White Pine Wolf Preserve liable for—including death—and it read like one of those commercials detailing the horrible side effects from certain medications.

Dahlia twisted at her ring. "I realize it looks daunting, but I'm sure you understand that most of those things will never happen. And we only need you until next week, as you can see from the dates. I'll be back then to help Rich."

I took a moment to digest the word Dahlia had used—*most*. *Most* of the things wouldn't happen. But if I signed the document, I was acknowledging that at least *one* of those injuries might occur, and why would I agree to that?

Dahlia looked at me expectantly, her hands clasped almost as if in prayer. Or was it desperation?

I was seriously considering bolting out the door and running down the long driveway when Evie piped up.

"Thus far, no one has been injured at White Pine," she declared, her British accent lending an air of authority. "Everyone has trepidation when they sign, but please know that the contract had to be drafted to allow for every possible event, however unlikely."

I examined the dates again—as Dahlia had promised on the phone, they only needed me for eight days. Surely I could handle that short a period of time and walk away uninjured. Besides, if I didn't help Rich, he would have to work overtime at the preserve, and then he couldn't come through for his daughter.

I literally felt like I was signing my life away, but I scrawled my name on the blank line and slid the contract back to Evie.

"Thank you so very much," Dahlia said, patting my hand. "You won't regret your time with the wolves. They're quite intuitive, you know. They have a way of lifting the spirits." She stood. "Evie, I feel like we need to go over my schedule one more time."

Evie nodded, then turned my way. "See you in the morning, say around seven-thirty, Belinda?"

I knew I had been dismissed, so I agreed and said my good-byes. I made my way outside, texting Red as I walked. He said he was actually not far away and he would arrive in about ten minutes, so I settled into a rocking chair, wishing the sky hadn't turned so gray and overcast.

In no time at all, Red pulled the shiny black car up next to me and parked. He jumped out to open the door, giving me a raised-eyebrow look that spoke volumes. I didn't feel like explaining why I'd be returning to this place, so I slid onto the cool leather seat and stayed silent all the way home. Red seemed to respect my privacy. The only thing he asked was if I'd need a ride in the morning. I reluctantly said I did, so we set up a pickup time.

I unlocked my front door, then dropped my boots on the mat. I hung my sweatshirt on a peg in the hall closet. Trudging down to the bathroom, I shoved my mud-splattered socks and jeans into the laundry basket.

After pulling on a pair of yoga pants that were probably more comfy than flattering, I knew I had to talk to someone, since I was about to burst.

And there was only one person I felt like talking to.

My sister, Katrina, was one of the most insightful psychologists out there, and she had a knack of knowing exactly what I needed to hear in nearly every situation. Although I tended to balk at actually *taking* her advice, she was the one I called when I felt overwhelmed in life.

Katrina listened none too quietly as I explained about White Pine and my contract, interjecting *hmph*s and growly noises as I spoke. I wasn't sure if she was upset about my situation or just uncomfortable since she'd been placed on bed rest a week ago.

"Hang on," she said. I heard her fingers flying over her laptop keys. "I found a couple more recent instances of wolf fatalities—both from wolves in captivity, BB."

I appreciated her concern—evident by the use of her favorite nickname for me—but I could also tell when she was blowing smoke.

"Define *more recent*," I said.

"Well, you know, in the grand scheme of things, they're recent," she hedged.

"When?" I demanded.

"The eighties and nineties for the ones in captivity." She rushed on. "The point is that sometimes they attack in captivity. Why do you think that contract was so extensive?"

I sighed. "I'll watch my back, sis. After all, they did give me pepper spray, so I won't be totally helpless. But I can't back out of this now. They're counting on me."

"They always are," she said, grunting like she was shifting positions. "Just think of the wolves as wild, not pets. Anyway, you'd better be alive when this baby arrives, so you can spoil him rotten."

I grinned as I thought of the little guy who would soon come into the world and take on the name his parents had chosen—Jasper Drew Morris. Drew was our dad's name, and he was beside himself when he'd found out Katrina and Tyler were naming his first grandson after him.

"Oh, I'll be around," I promised. "Besides, who else is going to teach Jasper how to snowmobile?"

* * * *

By the next morning, I felt more stoked about the adventure at hand. I'd done my own online research, and the majority of wolf killings seemed to occur in cases of starvation or rabies. Yes, there were the odd wolves-in-captivity attacks, but they certainly weren't the norm.

I'd also remembered that Shaun had said they sometimes allowed wolves to roam around the visitors during tours. While that probably meant Dahlia's insurance was astronomical, it also meant that she trusted the beasts enough to allow them around random people—maybe even children.

It had taken some time, but in typical fashion, my spontaneous nature had overcome my misgivings. I was pretty sure that same spontaneous nature also kept my parents up at nights, but I tried not to dwell on it.

Red exuded displeasure when he picked me up, but he managed to maintain a poker face while driving to the preserve.

"My Volvo will be ready soon," I said. "I can walk over to pick it up this evening, so you won't have to take me to work tomorrow. Thanks for driving me around, though."

He glanced at me in the rearview mirror and gave a brief nod. Red was generally talkative, but today he'd taken a page out of my book and remained silent. I turned my attention out the window, noting how green everything was this time of year. I loved the spaciousness of Greenwich, which seemed a rare treat after my years in a studio apartment in Manhattan.

As we pulled into the parking lot, Rich strode out to meet me, neon vest in hand. He said hello to Red, who seemed to be sizing him up as if they were about to head into the gladiator ring together. After chatting about the warming weather, Red instructed Rich to keep a close eye on me. His tone implied that if Rich failed to protect me, there'd be some sort of retaliation that didn't fall within the bounds of my contract.

Rich readily agreed, so Red shook his hand and climbed into the car. As Red pulled away, Evie came outside and joined us. She reported that Dahlia had flown out of La Guardia during the night and would likely land in Arizona sometime within the next hour. She offered me fresh coffee, but since I'd downed two cups to keep my moxie up for this job, I politely refused.

I pulled my vest on, patted my pocket to make sure the pepper spray canister was there, then looked at Rich.

He seemed to sense my resolve. "Let's load up," he said, walking to a small shed that held the wheelbarrow and buckets. Something inside me was soothed when I saw that the buckets had been thoroughly cleaned.

Rich stuffed vitamin supplements into a few steaks and loaded them up. Unwilling to touch pounds of raw, unidentified meats with my bare hands, I politely asked Rich if there were any disposable gloves available. I didn't care if the wolves detected the latex scent; I just didn't want to smell like food. He didn't question me and motioned to a box of gloves on the wall. I quickly pulled on a pair, and together we packed the rest of the meat.

When we finally rolled up to the first double gate, I couldn't hide my trepidation. My hands were trembling.

Rich took notice. "All you'll need to do is water the wolves. I've been hand-feeding them forever, and it's no trouble for me to handle that end of it." He pointed. "There's a spigot above the trough, just inside the gate. You can fill the trough about halfway."

"Sure," I said. My voice cracked.

Rich opened the gate and we passed through, then he closed it behind us with a slam.

I steadied my hands and attempted to steady my spirit. Without looking around, I walked directly to the watering trough. Rich murmured to the animals, then meat began slapping against a metal pan.

As the wolves started eating, I could hear them crunching into bones. I don't know what I'd expected—after all, the meats hadn't been boneless—but it was an unnerving experience nonetheless.

As water filled the trough, I pivoted so I could covertly watch the action. One thicker-bodied wolf had finished eating, and the other two were vying for the remaining food. The slim brown wolf seemed to be the same one that had observed me from its rocky perch yesterday.

Rich wheeled over my way, the chubby gray and white wolf playing at his heels. "This one's Thor," he explained. "He looks like a bear, but he's a softie. He's a German shepherd and wolf mix. His original owners couldn't handle him. He's become the alpha of this pack."

Thor frolicked his way over to me, took a brief sniff, then returned to the feeding bowl. The other two wolves split up—one heading into the woods, and one moving my way with alarming speed.

"Which wolf is that?" I asked, pointing to the thin brown one who was charging my way.

Rich patted the wolf's back as it raced past him. "Don't worry—just keep talking with me and don't look at her. Her name's Freya, and she's a survivor."

The lanky wolf stopped by my side and started sniffing at my jeans. I ignored her, trying to focus on the conversation. "What do you mean, a survivor?"

Rich's gaze darkened. "Freya was bred to fight. Most of her early years were spent chained to a tree. She has more scars than any living animal ought to have."

Anger and compassion shot through me, and it was almost as if the wolf picked up on it. She nudged her wet, white-scarred nose into my hand, then dropped onto the ground at my feet and rolled over, exposing her stomach, which was also hideously scarred.

"She likes you," Rich said.

Automatically, I leaned down to pet Freya's stomach, carefully running my hands over the puckered lines of her scars. The wolf kicked her leg and seemed to give me a side smile.

Thor and the other wolf had gotten into some kind of tussle over a bone, yipping and snarling. Rich signaled that it was time to leave, so I turned off the water and gave Freya one last pat. She slunk off toward her favored rocky outcropping, and the fighting wolves stopped for a moment to watch her. I zipped ahead of Rich, and we were out of the gate in seconds.

As Thor and his frisky friend trotted closer to Freya, I hesitated. "Is she going to be okay?"

Rich chuckled. "Oh, sure. That's a mild fight—they scrap around nearly every day. Freya can hold her own, trust me."

I felt more confident as we made our way to the second enclosure. Rich instructed me to fill the watering trough again, and I appreciated the way he was letting me ease into my role.

The double gates came into view. Since I was in front, I slowed for Rich to wheel his way closer.

I glanced at the enclosure, trying to locate the trough. But my gaze settled on something else—something that was utterly disturbing.

Just inside the second gate, it was plain to see that Njord, the white pack leader, had red stains all over his beautiful coat. He was standing sentry over something—no, *someone.*

Someone in a neon-green vest.

4

As if drawn by some devilish force, I bolted toward the gates. Rich didn't waste time dropping the wheelbarrow and racing toward my side. Together, we closed in on the gruesome scene, stopping short outside the first gate.

The poor person was mauled so badly, I couldn't even make out the face. But given the larger size of the body and the tennis shoes I recognized from yesterday, I knew who it was.

Shaun Fowler appeared to be dead.

I gave a reflexive gag. Shaun had been so helpful, so openly appreciative of my gaming skills. Why had he gone into the wolf enclosure in the first place? Had he made a habit of petting the animals before tours?

Rich was already pulling out his phone. "I'm calling for help. There's no way we can get any closer to check on Shaun. Once a wolf places something in its mouth, that object belongs to the wolf. Even with pepper spray, we don't want to try to get between the pack and something they think is theirs."

I kept an eye on Njord as Rich talked to emergency services. The white wolf had sunk to a sitting position next to Shaun's body, but the other two wolves had appeared on the scene. The tan fur under their chins also looked darkened and sticky, so I was guessing that all three animals had taken part in the killing.

I gagged again just about the time Veronica popped over a nearby knoll. She took one look at me and asked, "What's going on?"

Before I could answer, Carson, like some kind of bespectacled puppy, came trailing along behind Veronica. He looked over at Rich, who was in an intense phone conversation.

Carson pushed his glasses up his nose. "Is something wrong?"

I gestured weakly toward the wolves, unable to put things into words. Veronica stepped closer to the gate and gave a loud gasp.

Carson followed her, then stopped short and screeched. "Is that Shaun? Shaun Fowler? What happened? He's here way too early—he didn't have a tour until later this morning. We have to get help!"

Rich hung up and motioned for silence. "Carson, the police are on their way. It's too late for us to help Shaun. But I'm sure you would agree that your mother would want us to stay calm in this situation."

I nodded in agreement, hoping Carson would simmer down. His little freak-out was only making everything worse.

Carson seemed to rally. "You're so right. Mom would want me to step up and keep things running smoothly. I'll head back and let Evie know there was a wolf attack. Come with me, V."

Veronica's glossy lips twitched into a frown. "I told you, it's *Veronica.* And I'll stick around here, thanks."

I watched as Carson marched toward the visitors' center on his self-imposed mission.

Veronica went over to Rich and patted his arm. I sank down onto a large rock, unable to look toward the enclosure in case the wolves had started to chew on Shaun again.

It seemed to take forever, but finally a police officer and another man made their way toward us. As they got closer, I realized that the second man was an animal control officer.

One cop and one animal control officer to three man-eating wolves seemed a poor ratio.

Rich stepped over and began talking with the police officer, who looked thoroughly disturbed by the attack. I glanced at Veronica, who was staring into the enclosure with an almost morbid fascination. Her thesis had just gotten real, in the most horrifying way ever.

The police officer nodded toward us, introducing himself as Sergeant Jacob Hardy. He said we needed to stick around for questions, but his first priority was to get the body out of the enclosure.

Rich led the two men toward the gate, and after some brief back-and-forth, Sergeant Hardy unsheathed his gun. The animal control officer also retrieved a gun with a long, thin barrel that I assumed contained a knockout dart or something along those lines. Rich unlocked the first fence, shouting to shoo the wolves away from the body. The animals responded with a few weak yips, then they split up and trotted off to observe from a safe distance. From the covert way they watched the intruders, it was clear they had some idea of what guns were. Had any of them seen guns before, or could they instinctively feel they were in mortal danger?

After a brief examination, Sergeant Hardy must have pronounced Shaun dead, because he pulled a body bag from his rucksack. As the men proceeded to wrestle Shaun's chewed-on remains into the bag, I had to look away again.

Veronica, however, watched with widened eyes. Although she was likely in shock, she gave off the vibe of being more fearful than sad about Shaun's death. I found her hard to relate to. Shaun had been such a friendly guy, the kind of person everyone would have liked, and now his life had been cut dreadfully short. Surely Veronica knew what a blow this would be to his family, since she was probably close to his age.

As the men came out, locking both gates behind them, I finally started to breathe normally again. Other officers had arrived on the scene. Two of them carried the body bag back to the visitors' center, while others began to tape off the area and take pictures.

I stayed seated as Veronica edged over toward Sergeant Hardy, probably anxious to get the scoop.

The sergeant pulled out hand sanitizer and passed it over to Rich and the animal control officer.

Rich thanked him, a thoughtful look on his face. "Those wolves are hungry. That shouldn't be the case."

"Looked like some kind of feeding frenzy to me," Sergeant Hardy said.

The animal control officer was grim. "If it had been a true feeding frenzy, they wouldn't have left as much of him."

Rich gave a reluctant nod of agreement. "Oddest thing I ever saw. Doesn't make sense. He hadn't even pulled his pepper spray."

Sergeant Hardy stared at Rich. "He had pepper spray?"

"We all do—in the vest pockets."

The sergeant nodded. "I'll make note of that and find out if it was on him. There's also the possibility that it malfunctioned—but in that case, he probably would have dropped it nearby."

Veronica leaned into the conversation. "I'd be happy to answer your questions," she interjected. "We came along just after Rich and Belinda found him."

I had the sinking feeling that Veronica was going to pump the sergeant for information—information she could use for writing her thesis.

As Sergeant Hardy turned his full attention to Veronica, the wolves converged on their bloodstained massacre site. A fresh wave of nausea swept over me.

I closed my eyes as Veronica droned on for a while. When she finally stopped talking, I slowly cracked my eyelids and peered out.

Sergeant Hardy towered in front of me, a solemn look on his face. "Excuse me, but are you Belinda? Would you mind answering a few quick questions?"

"I don't mind. No problem. And my full name is Belinda Blake," I noted.

He extended a strong hand and helped me to my feet, then he pulled out a small notebook and a pencil.

"I understand you're a new employee here?"

"Yes, I just started today, actually."

He asked me several different ways if I'd noticed anything strange about this wolf pack—as if I knew what a normal wolf pack looked like. He seemed to be growing more agitated with my vague answers, and finally he asked pointedly, "But why would you want to work at a place like this?"

That seemed quite unprofessional, even downright hateful, toward Dahlia's legitimate place of business. I assured him that the owner and employees had seemed competent when I'd signed on for the job. I further shared that Shaun had been quite friendly with Njord just yesterday.

Sergeant Hardy's lips were set in a forbidding line, his animosity thinly veiled.

I decided to make an educated guess and asked a question of my own. "Has something like this happened before at White Pine?"

Sergeant Hardy opened his mouth as if he wanted to answer, but two officers jogged over and began to fill him in on tasks they had completed. The sergeant waved me away, so I walked over to Rich, who still lingered by the fence line.

"I'm so sorry you had to see this, and on your first day here," Rich said. "This never should have happened."

"I agree." I wished I could walk off the preserve and never return, but everyone would be stretched even thinner with one tour guide down and Dahlia in Arizona. Plus, I had signed the contract. If I bailed on a pet-sitting job, it would certainly damage my reputation in Greenwich circles.

Rich rubbed at his short salt-and-pepper beard. "Listen, I know this has to be distressing for you. I have a daughter about your age, and she'd have run screaming from this place the moment she saw Shaun's body. You're one tough cookie, Belinda. Why don't you head back to the visitors' center, have some coffee, and I'll figure out some work you can do that'll keep you away from the wolves the rest of the day."

I could've thrown my arms around the thoughtful older man. Instead, I struggled to hold back sudden tears and mumbled a thanks. None too steadily, I walked down the path toward the visitors' center.

As the barn came into view, it was obvious that the preserve had been thrown into an uproar. A sleek tour bus sat in the corner of the parking lot, and a small crowd milled around it. One woman with bleach-blonde hair was snapping bubbles with her gum and complaining loudly about the holdup with their tour, while a diminutive man ineffectively patted at her shoulder. Evie and the tour guide were having a heated conversation just outside the visitors' center door. There was a *Closed* sign on the gift shop, probably so visitors couldn't ramble around while Evie was dealing with the fallout of the canceled tour.

How many tours had Shaun booked for today? Regardless of the number, I was certain the police would have Evie cancel them. Dahlia would probably have to refund all the tour groups.

In other words, Shaun's death was going to cost her.

In an attempt to avoid the restless crowd, I headed for the side door and went straight into the kitchen. Thick, burned brew sat in the coffeepot, so I dumped it, guessing at measurements to make a fresh pot.

A man with thick graying hair strode into the side door, dropping a glance at me as he walked toward the gift store. Befuddled as to who the bold newcomer was, I stood.

"Excuse me, sir. I believe the shop is closed."

The man whirled to stare at me through thick glasses lenses. "I'm sorry. I should've introduced myself first. I'm Dennis Arden, Dahlia's father-in-law." He extended a hand and I gave it a brief shake. "I stop by every now and again to see how things are going—I live about fifteen minutes away," he said.

"Oh, I see. I'm sorry. I just wasn't sure, what with the crowd out there—"

"I totally understand. I haven't been able to get hold of Evie to let her know I was dropping in, then I saw the hubbub and figured something was up. Do you know what's going on?"

I hated to be the bearer of ghastly news, but Dennis would likely hear what happened sooner rather than later. Still, I figured I should keep the details to a minimum. "A tour guide was found dead today," I answered.

He held out a hand, as if warding off my words. "Found dead? But where? Who was it?"

It was inevitable he would ask, but I wasn't sure how much information we were allowed to share. "It was here at the preserve, and it was Shaun Fowler," I offered, my voice cracking.

Dennis looked appalled. "Yes, I'd met that young man. He seemed a rather enterprising sort." His nostrils flared. "And from the look on your face, I'm betting he didn't die of natural causes. It was those danged wolves, am I right?"

Dennis shifted on his feet. He wasn't the only one thoroughly upset by Shaun's death, but he was acting like he wanted to spit nails.

"I'm afraid that's correct," I said, trying to keep my voice soft.

"This whole preserve is a joke," Dennis blurted. "Why my son decided to let his crazy ex use his land, I'll never know. Maybe because she needed a place to live. But, of course, it was her harebrained idea to build this wolf zoo. Dumbest thing I ever heard of, trying to rehabilitate animals that have been so badly abused. It's asking for trouble—I warned her someone was going to get killed someday." He sighed. "Oh well, Quinn should've never married that free-spirited hippie in the first place."

I didn't know Dahlia well, but I felt Dennis wasn't giving her a fair shake. After all, Shaun had mentioned that Dahlia was a hard worker, pouring many hours into rehabbing the wolves. She'd set up the preserve in hopes of doing good, and probably as a means of making income for her family.

It wasn't right of Dennis to slam his ex-daughter-in-law behind her back. I put my hands on my hips in an attempt to stop his tirade. "I think it's admirable. Besides, I'm sure this preserve helps provide for your grandson."

Dennis huffed. "Carson? That boy won't amount to a hill of beans. He's too much like his mother."

I couldn't imagine my doting grandma ever speaking of me that way, like I was some unwanted nuisance. I mentally added Dennis's name to my Most-Disliked-on-the-Preserve list. The list already included Carson and Veronica.

I was trying to come up with a sufficiently smug retort when Evie burst into the gift shop. As I glanced out the kitchen door, it was clear to see the usually peppy administrative assistant was teary-eyed.

"I need to talk with her," Dennis said, stalking out of the kitchen. I hoped he didn't plan to blast Evie with his angry diatribe.

It seemed the only thing I could do to help Evie was to keep busy with my own chores. I sucked down the last dregs of my barely passable coffee, making a mental note to bring my hazelnut creamer in the morning, *if* I decided to come back to work—contract or no contract.

5

Trying to ignore the rumble of Dennis's raised voice, I pulled on my sweatshirt. After topping my bulky look with the bright green vest, I trudged out the kitchen door. I was thankful to find Rich spraying down feed buckets near a red storage building, so I didn't have to go back into the woods to look for him.

He cut the sprayer as I approached. "Feeling a little better?"

My run-in with Dennis Arden hadn't been quite the pick-me-up I'd needed, but I didn't want to bring Rich down with my negative observations. "Yes. I made fresh coffee, if you want some."

"I'm not a coffee drinker, but thanks. I'll be heading in for lunch soon. You feel ready for another job?"

I gave an unconvincing nod.

"Don't worry, I'm keeping you away from the wolf enclosures. If you don't mind feeding the smaller farm animals, I can head back to the wolves and start brushing them out, since their winter coats are already starting to shed."

"Did Sergeant Hardy say you're allowed to go back in there by yourself?" I asked, anxious for the kind man's safety.

"I'm just doing what I have to do to keep this place running," Rich said, avoiding my question. "I'm not afraid of those wolves."

He didn't elaborate, so I didn't press him. He did have pepper spray, and from all I'd seen, Rich was pretty instinctive about the animals in his care. He wasn't likely to risk his life just to brush the wolves' fur.

Once Rich had explained what I should feed the animals, I walked over to the expansive yard stretching behind Dahlia's house, where the smaller pets were kept.

The chicken coop was a pretty good size. Dahlia was raising some unusual breeds, as well as some of the more standard ones, like Rhode Island Reds. I fed them first, then gathered a few eggs from their nests. Latching the gate closed behind me, I nestled the eggs into the grass to pick up later, although I was unsure what I was supposed to do with them.

I made my way to the fenced peacock area. The regal birds were a sight to behold, but they made earsplitting screeches the entire time I was in their fence. They seemed more interested in me than in the cracked oats I fed them.

From there, I headed over to the goat herd. The animals were fearless, nudging at me and vying for my attention with loud bleats as I refreshed their water supply. As always, I was entranced by goats' unique sideways pupils. My mom had kept a few goats when I was younger, and I'd always enjoyed their creative and relentless efforts to escape. Mom hadn't enjoyed their antics nearly so much, and had sold them off.

By the time I'd finished my chores, the sun was covered by clouds and a chilly wind had picked up. I carefully placed the eggs in my sweatshirt pocket before heading back to the visitors' center. Glancing at the parking lot, I saw that the tour bus was gone and only a couple of cars remained. I texted Red, and he said he'd be over in fifteen minutes.

Inside, Evie was busy reorganizing an eye-catching display table that needed no adjustments. Her British accent seemed heavier as she greeted me. "Oh, my dear Belinda. It's dreadful that your first day was like this. Sergeant Hardy told me to cancel all the tours for the week, and I have, but I'm completely at loose ends as to what to do with myself now. I'm no good at feeding the animals, or I would help you. I grew up in the city, you see. The wolves know I'm terrified of them." Tears welled in her dark-lashed blue eyes. "My mum said this was a rubbish job for me to take on, but I didn't listen. Dahlia convinced me I'd be a huge help to her. Now everything's gone wonky, and I can't reach Dahlia on her mobile and—"

I cut her off with a quick hug. "It'll be fine. Rich and I can handle things with the wolves. You just concentrate on keeping the business end running." A thought occurred to me. "Wasn't Carson supposed to be helping you while his mom was away? Where is he?"

Evie shrugged. "I haven't seen him since this morning, when he told me about Shaun's death. I was so gobsmacked I barely paid attention to where he went. Most likely he's been holed up in his house—it's where he stays most of the time, pecking about on his computer as if he's doing something important."

I wondered what, if any, computer business Carson did, but it was evident that he wasn't contributing much to the management of his mother's preserve. His efforts thus far seemed to be comprised of taking long walks in the same direction as Veronica, as well as poking his nose into other people's business.

The ironic thing was that his disdainful grandpa, Dennis Arden, seemed to share his trait of nosing around where he wasn't really wanted.

When I asked Evie where to put the eggs, she went into the kitchen and absently handed me a plastic bowl. After placing them in the bowl and setting it in the fridge, I turned back to say good-bye. Evie's chin was trembling, as if she might burst into tears. I gave her another hug and a pat on the back. She was definitely *gobsmacked*, as she'd put it, and she seemed very alone.

She probably needed to talk about Shaun's death, but we weren't really close enough for that yet. Besides, she'd acted so strangely yesterday, sneaking around with her phone like she was having an illegal conversation. I wasn't sure if I could trust her yet.

I placed my green vest on a wall peg and gave Evie a brief wave. "See you tomorrow," I said. "I'll be here at seven-thirty."

She sniffed, then nodded. "See you then."

Once I stepped outside, I heard someone rustling around in the red storage building. Rich came out of the building's metal doorway, holding a pitchfork.

He stopped and gave me a questioning look. "You coming back tomorrow?"

I only hesitated a moment, which really wasn't bad, given my current feelings toward the wolves. "Yes, I am."

Rich leaned on the pitchfork handle. "Good. You were a natural today. I know the wolves can be scary at first, but you handled it well."

Scary was hardly an adequate term for the way Njord had looked, standing there with blood splattered on his coat. I shivered and shoved my hands into my sweatshirt pocket.

"Thanks. And thanks for letting me tend to the other animals this afternoon."

He nodded and moseyed off to whatever task awaited him. I made my way to the only black car in the parking lot. Red jumped out and opened my door without saying a word. Once I was settled, he adjusted his mirror and looked at me.

"How was your day?" he asked.

My face made some strange crumpling movement, and I couldn't push words out. Instead of driving off, Red just sat there patiently with the car idling.

Finally, I was able to articulate something. "A tour guide died today. We found him in the wolf enclosure."

Red's expression shifted from disbelief to horror, then finally settled into outrage. "Surely you won't be going back, then?"

"I have to. They really are shorthanded and everything's so up in the air—"

"I'll be forced to report this to Mister Stone," Red said, and I knew he meant Stone the fifth.

"And why would you do that?" I asked. "There's no need to bother him over there in Bhutan."

Red shook his head as he pulled out. "I promised to keep him posted on any situations that could jeopardize your safety while he is gone."

I laughed. "What's he going to do about it? Assign you as my bodyguard on those dangerous jobs?"

Red didn't even smile.

My deepest suspicions rose to the surface. "Red...what exactly *is* your job title?"

He ignored my question. "Should I drop you at the garage so you can pick up your car?"

I'd forgotten all about that. "Sure, that would be great." I was tempted to add "*bodyguard*," but I restrained myself.

* * * *

The fully repaired Bluebell was running like a top as I pulled onto Putnam Avenue and grabbed supper from a drive-through. Usually, I'd take the time to cook something, but today every last bit of my emotional energy was spent. I just wanted to crash and play video games.

As I kicked back on the couch, indulging in a cherry Dr Pepper, I loaded up my new role-playing game. Companies sent me early copies for review, and so far, I'd really enjoyed the story world on this one. However, the moment I leveled up and found out I had to fight off wolves in an extremely realistic forest, I shut it down.

Maybe I'd play another day.

Maybe I wouldn't.

Adding to my despondency was the knowledge that Shaun had been the first of my avid gamer fans I'd ever met in real life. I could hardly imagine how Sergeant Hardy had informed Shaun's parents of what had happened—it was just so unthinkable. I supposed his parents could always try to sue Dahlia, but given the exhaustive terms of our employee contracts, I doubted they could win.

I grabbed the uneaten half of my chicken wrap, donned my coat, and walked around to my back patio. It was about forty-five degrees, but the sun was hitting the table straight-on, so heat radiated from it.

My daffodils provided colorful pockets of cheer against the monochromatic stone wall that lined my backyard. I was about to pick a bouquet when my cell phone rang.

It was Jonas.

I hesitated, letting it ring again. Should I tell him what had happened today? I hadn't even told my parents yet, but Katrina was calling tonight, so that meant I'd have to let them know before she did.

I picked up, still uncertain, but the moment Jonas said my name in his relaxed, assured voice, I decided to tell him about Shaun.

"Belinda, I'm glad I caught you. What's new? Your mom said you got a new job?"

I always thought it was adorable how my mom loved to talk up my accomplishments to every neighbor who would listen.

And Jonas always listened.

I briefly told him how I'd wound up with the unexpected wolf-sitting position. When Jonas didn't overreact, I went on to described my first day on the job—starting with the discovery of Shaun's body in the wolf enclosure.

Once I finished speaking, there was complete silence. I asked Jonas if he was still on the line.

He cleared his throat. "Yes, I'm here. So what's next? Are you going back or quitting?"

I liked that he didn't assume I would have immediately turned in my resignation. "I'm going back. Dahlia couldn't find anyone else to fill in, and Rich has to get a house ready for his daughter, who's getting married soon, so he doesn't have time—"

"It's okay—you don't have to explain things to me. I was just thinking… I'll be heading down to New York City early Saturday morning. I have quite a bit of honey and maple syrup to sell at a Brooklyn green market. I've booked a bed-and-breakfast for Saturday night, since I planned to sell until the end of the day. But I'll be free that evening. You want me to swing by your place?"

It was at least a one-hour "swing" from Brooklyn to Greenwich, but it would be a delight to show Jonas around the posh town and my little carriage house. Although his words were casual, like he didn't care if I agreed to a visit or not, there was a barely discernible note of hopefulness in his voice that gave me a little thrill.

I could hardly temper my excitement. "Of course! I'd love that! Saturday evening? And don't eat supper. I want to feed you."

He laughed. "No arguments here. I'm sure I'll be hungry from peddling my wares all day, and I know what a great cook you are. I still remember that stuffed chicken you brought over when Mom was getting radiation." His voice grew serious. "But are you sure you want to stick it out with this wolf-sitting job? Of course, you're not a newb to animal life since your dad's a vet—that's one of the things I like about you—but do they make you feed the wolves by yourself?"

His "one of the things I like about you" comment swept like an electric charge down my spine. Jonas wasn't the type to throw compliments around, so when he did, I knew it wasn't idle flattery.

I groped around for an answer to the question I hardly recalled. "Um, yeah. I mean, no. Today I did the water while Rich fed the wolves, so I wasn't alone in the enclosure. Then, after we found Shaun, I just fed the hobby farm animals and didn't go back into the wolf fences." I tried to cover my wordy fumblings. "Speaking of your mom, how's she doing?"

Although Jonas's mom had finished chemo and radiation for her stage three breast cancer late last year, I hadn't heard if there were more treatments on the horizon. Jonas was his mom's primary caregiver, since he was the one to move into the family farmhouse a few years ago when his dad had died.

There was a pregnant pause. My stomach clenched as I realized what he was probably going to say.

"It didn't work," he said simply. "It's spread."

Tears rolled down my cheeks as I recalled all the times I'd visited Naomi Hawthorne's house on errands for my mom. Naomi always had me sit down over a cup of coffee and a freshly baked goodie so we could chat about whatever happened to be weighing on my mind. She had a stillness and a patient way about her that pulled me in, unlike my perpetually enterprising mom.

I groped for words. "I'm so sorry...be sure to call my parents if you need help with anything."

"We will." His voice lightened, and he asked how my book club reading was going. Our classic this month was *The Great Gatsby*, which had thankfully been a short and nondemanding read, given my new job.

"I don't like Daisy Buchanan," I said.

"You wouldn't," he responded.

"She's so…"

"Helpless? Fake? Manipulative?"

"I don't know. Just *boring*. It's like she can't commit, you know? Either stay with your ogre husband or leave him for the enigmatic yet adoring man from your past. Don't be so wishy-washy."

Jonas chuckled. "If there's one thing you're not, Belinda Jade Blake, it's wishy-washy."

It was disarming and kind of enchanting to hear Jonas use my full name. *Jade* was my mom's nature-loving homage to her favorite stone, and oddly enough, it had stirred my interest in rocks and gemstones. Dad always told me that my eyes were the same color as jade. When I was a teen, he'd given me a jade bracelet, encouraging me to start a collection. Since then, I had accumulated several unusual jade pieces when I was in the Peace Corps in China and during my other travels.

Katrina's middle name was Pearl, and she wasn't crazy about it. Still, she was going to name her firstborn Jasper, so maybe subconsciously she was carrying on our family gemstone-naming tradition.

We talked a little more about Gatsby, then Jonas's mom called to him, so he said good-bye. After I hung up, I stared at the expectant, blinking light on my game system. I couldn't return to the wolf game tonight. Although I had review article deadlines looming, it would be best if I took a long bath and tried to relax. Maybe I could fix a cup of hot chocolate with liberal amounts of spray whip and a sprinkle of cinnamon. I'd smooth on my new caramel-scented lotion and slip into my comfiest pj's.

I didn't know who I was trying to kid. There was no way I'd get much sleep after a day like today.

6

I groaned when my phone alarm played a charming little tune designed to assure me that today would be carefree and beautiful. I had my serious doubts.

However, by the time I slid onto Bluebell's tan leather seat and started her up, the sun was out and it was fifty degrees. Bluebell sprang to life and her engine almost purred, she was running so smoothly. I slapped her dashboard and told her she was my favorite.

What would Stone think if he knew I talked to my car? What would Jonas think?

And why did I care what either one of them thought? If I wanted to talk to Bluebell, by Jove, I'd talk to Bluebell.

I picked up a large cup of Dunkin' D, so I was feeling even more sassy as I pulled up the long drive to the wolf preserve. I found myself wishing I wouldn't see Carson, Veronica, or Dennis Arden today, since all three of them seemed to push my buttons.

Thankfully, I ran into Rich first. He was watering the pansies in the window boxes and turned to greet me with a smile.

"Good to see you. Beautiful day, isn't it?"

I didn't know if I could ever refer to any day on this now-tainted preserve as *beautiful*, but I capitulated. "It's great to finally have some warmer weather, for sure. If you want to hang on a sec, I'll just run in and throw my lunch in the fridge and grab my vest, then I'll be right out to help you."

"Sure thing."

Evie was nowhere to be seen, even though someone had flipped the visitors' center sign to *Open*. I hustled into the kitchen and shoved my lunch bag into the stainless-steel fridge, trying not to look at the off-white fridge standing next to it. I hoped against hope that Rich wouldn't make me feed the wolves, but if he did ask me to do it, could I really refuse? I had signed the contract, after all, and if I shirked on my duties, Dahlia wouldn't give me a good referral when I left. I needed all the positive reviews I could gather in Greenwich society.

I slowly pulled on my vest, steeling myself for whatever chores Rich assigned me. I doubted he'd send me into the wolf enclosure alone; besides, he would surely know how to handle the animals if they got too unruly.

Evie rose from behind the counter when I came out, and I realized she'd been there all along, just hunkered down where I couldn't see her. It was almost like she'd been hiding.

I took a second look at her, trying to figure out what she was up to. She was dressed, coiffed, and made-up so perfectly, I got the impression she'd donned her armor for the day. The woman looked like she'd stepped off the Paris runway.

She didn't initiate conversation, which was odd. She had struck me as quite an extroverted extrovert.

"Hi," I said, cutting the awkward silence. "Did you ever reach Dahlia?"

"I finally did. They don't have much Wi-Fi on the preserve she's visiting. Anyway, the soonest flight she could catch was this evening, so she'll be back tomorrow. Sergeant Hardy recommended she come as soon as possible, because he's releasing the story to the news tonight."

We both had a moment of silence, fully aware that reporters would likely be crawling all over the place by morning.

"Are you working on paperwork today?" I probed.

"What? Oh, no. I was just…straightening some things." Her eyes darted to the window. "In fact, I need to get back to it now."

She ducked behind the desk, making herself invisible again.

I took a glance out the window, but no one was out there. Evie was definitely in a clandestine mode for some reason, but maybe she was like me and was trying to avoid interactions with certain people. I didn't have time to sit around and speculate on the motivations for her behavior.

"Okay, well, 'bye," I said, then walked outside. Rich had already pulled out the wheelbarrow and buckets, so it looked like I'd be joining him for wolf-feeding duties once again. Neither Jonas nor my family would be happy to know I was heading back into the enclosures.

But if Rich could do it, so could I. He also shouldn't be going in there alone, and we were the only ones handling chores around here. I grabbed a pair of disposable gloves and followed him to the side door.

He gave me a grateful smile as he propped the kitchen door open. He started passing the meats to me. I'd gotten more proficient at loading the buckets, and in no time at all, we were poised to head back into the woods.

"You'll be on water duty again, if that's okay," he said. "I'll handle the food."

"Thank you." While I didn't really want to go back in with the wolves, at least I wouldn't have to act as the animals' waitress, hand-delivering their food.

When Rich pushed the gates open at Thor's enclosure, Freya was the first to approach—and she headed straight for me. Her head was lowered and her tail wagged as she careened into my shins and started rubbing around my legs.

Rich was making his way to the wolves' metal dish, but he turned. "You okay?"

"Sure, yeah." I turned on the water, hoping Freya would be distracted by the sound of her meal dropping into the dish. But even as Thor and the other wolf swirled around the food, Freya stayed firmly planted at my side.

Almost like she was protecting me.

Did she sense my increased anxiety? It was definitely possible. Or maybe she was looking for comfort herself. I stole glances at the crooked white scars on her nose. She had a kind of imperfect, tragic beauty.

I looked over at Rich. Thor had finished gobbling his own food. The beefy wolf-dog shoved his muzzle into Rich's outstretched hand, clearly demanding attention. Rich scratched Thor's ears and rubbed his rump, talking to him all the while. Thor sank into a blissful heap on the ground.

Freya wasn't nearly as forward as Thor, but she'd positioned herself at my feet, making it difficult for me to move. I had to admit, this wolf was really growing on me. "Think of the wolves as wild, not pets," Katrina had warned. Yet these animals acted so much like domesticated dogs, I had to keep reminding myself of that fact.

I cut the water when the trough was half full, and Freya obligingly stood to let me pass. As we moved out of the enclosure with no incident, I let out a relieved sigh.

"They're not killers." Rich's voice was firm as he rattled on ahead of me, the wheelbarrow wheel bouncing.

"But the wolves in Njord's pack are," I responded sharply.

He shot me a grim look. "I still can't believe it. I've worked with those wolves from the time we got them. And Njord—I was there when he was born."

I hurried to catch up to Rich, unsure if I'd heard him correctly. "You worked with them from the start? Along with Dahlia, right? Shaun told me how she'd spent so much time getting them acclimated and all that."

Something flared in Rich's eyes. "Sure, Dahlia *tells* everyone what a godsend she is to these broken, unwanted animals, but in reality, she's played little part in their day-to-day lives. She buys them, then leaves the rest to me. I'm the one who integrates the wolves into the packs. I'm the one who feeds them. I'm the one who watches for signs of illness. Dahlia might pretend to be some kind of wolf-savior, but to be honest, I'm betting the wolves would hardly recognize her."

I lagged behind, stunned into silence. Why would Dahlia tell such outright lies to Shaun and others, taking credit for what Rich had done? What was the point of starting a wolf preserve if you didn't really care about wolves?

Unless she was making really good money from it, which I couldn't imagine, given the amount she was charging for tours. Maybe the wolf preserve was just a front...like a money laundering operation? Maybe Evie was acting all nervous because she knew the IRS was watching them?

I shook my head. I had been watching too many spy shows. Since when did the IRS make spying house calls? Money laundering probably didn't occur in real life as often as it did on TV, especially in an affluent town like Greenwich.

Still, it wasn't beyond the realm of possibility. I would watch Dahlia closely when she returned to see if she even interacted with the wolves.

If she didn't...ugh. That probably meant she hadn't really planned on helping Rich when she returned, which meant she would have to ask me to extend my contract.

I stared at Rich's back, knowing I couldn't leave the poor man alone on chore duty so close to his daughter's wedding. His highest priority was to finish the floors for her, so that she and her new husband could move into their home with minimal delays.

Rich shoved the wheelbarrow up a little incline and I picked up the pace. The second enclosure came into view.

The enclosure where Shaun had been mauled and partially eaten.

I cast about for some kind of conversation that would take my mind off our impending duties, but I wound up returning to the revelation Rich had just shared. "So...you don't think anything's off with Dahlia's business, do you? I mean, why would she invest so much in something that she's not even interested in?"

Rich's jaw tightened, and he didn't answer. Instead, he strode up to the gates and quickly unlocked them.

Apparently, our discussion of Dahlia's business dealings was closed.

Njord sat just behind the second gate, his golden gaze fixed on us. Although his fur looked a bit cleaner—probably from Rich's brushing yesterday—it was still discolored enough to remind us of what he'd done. I was relieved when he trotted behind Rich toward the food bowl.

I walked straight toward the spigot. On my way, I noticed that the other two wolves in this enclosure—standard timber wolves, I'd guess—resembled each other so closely, they could be related. Maybe some family packs were allowed to stick together in captivity.

I was about to ask Rich about them when Njord snarled and snapped at the others. Rich backed up from the food bowl to give the animals space, but he didn't appear nervous. Sure enough, all three dove into the meat like it was their personal kill, with Njord commandeering the lion's share.

Rich walked over to me and hooked his thumbs into his belt loops. He gave me a keen look. "How are you *really* doing with all this?"

I thought about it. "Okay, I think."

For the moment, I actually believed it. Aside from their recent little spat over food, the wolves had seemed calmer and more satiated today. In fact, they were already meandering off without having eaten all their meat.

Then it hit me that they had probably eaten their fill of Shaun the day before. Bile rose in my throat.

"They're not even hungry," I said bitterly.

"It doesn't make sense," Rich agreed, not picking up on my disgusted tone. "I mean that they were so ravenous yesterday. I fed them after the police left, and they seemed abnormally hungry."

"Probably like they said, it was a sort of feeding frenzy."

"That really doesn't explain it. It's almost like there's an underlying cause—something I'm missing." Rich backtracked toward the gate, so I turned off the water and tagged along. As I passed Njord, he actually bumped his wet nose against my hand, but I couldn't imagine petting the same animal that might have killed Shaun. The wolf sat down as we went out the gate.

How likely was it that a wolf that had just tasted human flesh wouldn't turn around and try to attack another human? That he would act calm the next day, as if nothing had happened?

Like Rich said, something seemed off about the whole situation, but I couldn't figure out what it was.

7

Once again, Rich seemed to open up as we tromped through the woods. He began to elaborate on the misgivings he was having about the wolves' diet.

"I've been considering easing the wolves over to a feast-or-famine diet—it replicates what they would eat in the wild. What I'd do is haul in an animal carcass every three to five days and let them have at it. But after seeing how ravenous they were yesterday—Njord's pack, in particular—I won't be doing that anytime soon. There's no sense trying to treat them like they're in the wild when they're not. Most likely, they wouldn't even be able to survive out there."

I nodded, remembering what I'd read about wolves that had been bred in captivity.

"Anyway, as long as they're not getting overweight with our daily feeding schedule—which they aren't—I'll stick with that."

It sounded like Rich had done more than his share of wolf diet research. Of all the people who worked here, he seemed the most informed as to the wolf psyche, if there even *was* such a thing.

Things were quiet back at the visitors' center—too quiet, with all the tours canceled. Of course, canceling was the wisest course of action, but I wondered how this tourist lull would impact Dahlia's bank account.

Rich waved me on and said he was going to water the smaller animals, if I wouldn't mind feeding them after lunch. I agreed, then ducked out of the now-blazing sun into the cool semidarkness of the gift shop. A few candles flickered on tables, and it smelled pleasantly like a floral shop.

Evie walked over to greet me, looking just as primped as she did this morning. She motioned to a frosted glass drink dispenser and asked if I wanted a glass of lavender lemonade. She confessed she'd been so bored with no foot traffic, she'd gotten Dahlia's permission to use her ingredients to make her family-recipe lavender lemonade.

"You should see Dahlia's kitchen. Top-of-the-line everything," Evie gushed, seemingly back to her cheery self. "She remodeled it when she moved in—with her rich ex's money." She gave me a grin and poured my lemonade.

After I took my first sip, I couldn't help but sigh. "This is amazing!"

Veronica strode out of the kitchen, and I forced my smile not to falter. I didn't want to let my bad feelings for the grad student show.

"It *is* amazing," Veronica said, draining her glass. "Could you hit me up with another glass, Evie?"

As Evie poured, Veronica's gaze swept over me. Dressed in my work clothes, I felt about ten years older than the fresh-faced Veronica, who was in reality probably in her mid-twenties, like me. Well, I was turning twenty-seven in July, but I still felt younger.

"How's your second day going?" Veronica asked.

I wanted to say that she'd know if she ever turned her hand to some real work, but I dialed it back a little. "Pretty good so far. I'm surprised you came in today, since all the tours were canceled. Can you research without watching the wolves interact with the tourists?"

She nodded, sipping her icy lemonade.

Evie had fallen silent. She stared out the window again. Seriousness had replaced her previous buoyant mood. Her covert manner made me think she was about to stop, drop, and roll behind her desk.

"Yes, I can still take notes without tourists," Veronica said, drawing my attention back to her. "As a matter of fact, Rich said he would take me to see the wolves sometime this afternoon, in order for me to observe how they behave after..." Her voice trailed off.

"After they killed someone, you mean?" I asked bluntly.

The kitchen door slammed shut before Veronica could answer. Instead, she said, "Don't tell me—it's Carson. The guy has a sixth sense of when I'm around."

I leaned back and glanced into the kitchen, and sure enough, Veronica was right. I gave her a subtle nod, suddenly feeling like her conspirator.

Carson sauntered out, shoving his phone into his back pocket as he approached us. "Hi," he said gruffly.

I had no doubt his awkward efforts to socialize were entirely on behalf of Veronica, who had picked up an insulated wolf tumbler and was examining it carefully.

As Evie politely offered Carson a glass of lemonade, the visitors' center door swung open. We all turned to stare at the dark-haired, dark-eyed man in his forties who walked toward us.

Carson's lips twisted downward. It was intriguing that someone other than Veronica had actually garnered a response from him.

"Marco!" Evie called out, stepping out to meet him. "Come and have a glass of lavender lemonade."

The mysterious Marco helped himself to a glass, glanced over each of us, then extended a wide hand to me. "I don't believe we've met," he said. "I'm Marco Goretti. I'm the one who facilitated most of Dahlia's wolf rescues."

"Nice to meet you," I said.

Veronica abruptly smacked the wolf tumbler on the table, handed her empty lemonade glass to Evie, then stalked out without another word. She had doubtless wearied of Carson's hawk-like observations of her every move.

Carson had the good sense to give Veronica a couple of minutes' head start, but as expected, he charged out the front door not long after her dramatic exit.

I glanced at Marco and Evie, but they had fallen into a deep conversation. I wanted to know more about Marco Goretti, and Carson's irritated response to the man's appearance warranted investigation. I pushed the wooden gift shop door open and followed Carson.

"Hold up," I shouted at his back. He was rushing along toward the red storage building, so Veronica had probably headed that way.

He turned, peering at me through his clear plastic frames as if I were a complete stranger. The dude was completely distracted by Veronica. I'd certainly never been so hotly pursued by a guy. What on earth was it about Veronica, aside from her obvious good looks, that attracted him so strongly?

"Yes?" he asked curtly.

"I saw how you reacted to Marco," I said, jogging up to his side. "What's up with him?"

Carson huffed. "If you must know, my mother made his acquaintance at a charity event years ago. He's the one who encouraged her to build the preserve with his sob stories about the abandoned wolves."

"Wasn't that a noble thing to do, though?"

He gave a short, shrill laugh. "What my mother didn't know is that Marco has numerous connections to the underworld of wolf breeding and fighting."

"How did you find that out? Have you told your mom?" I demanded.

Just then, Veronica zigzagged up the hill toward the wolf enclosures, like she'd been watching for her chance to escape the storage building.

Carson didn't even bother to respond to me; he simply scurried off after her. I actually felt sorry for Veronica. It had to be nearly impossible to get much research done with her dogged admirer.

Still a bit confused as to Marco's current role at the wolf preserve, I returned to the visitors' center to grab a quick lunch. Marco and Evie were nowhere in sight, so I made my way to the kitchen, washed my hands, and pulled out my food. I'd packed leftover cheese tortellini and a chopped salad, and the hearty meal tasted good after the long morning.

I continued to ponder. Why had Marco stopped in while Dahlia was out of town? Had he found a new animal for her to adopt?

And where were Evie and Marco, anyway? The silence stretched thin and seemed to balance on the dusty threads of sunlight that converged on the table.

I cleaned up, then grabbed a final glass of lemonade before heading back out. Evie stood in the parking lot, waving good-bye to Marco, who was sitting behind the wheel of an older red truck. Whatever business he'd come about must have been concluded, then. Surely he and Evie weren't in on some kind of scheme together?

* * * *

I walked around to start my other chores, but they didn't go as smoothly as they had yesterday. The chickens were fractious, the male peacock would not get out of my way, and one of the goats actually head-butted my thigh so hard, I was going to wind up with a huge bruise.

I felt beat down by the time I headed back to the visitors' center, but I wanted to check in with Rich before I left for the day. As I stepped inside, the gift shop was empty, so I walked over to check the kitchen. No one was around. Had Evie already gone home?

I reluctantly trudged toward the woods, figuring I'd find Rich there. Although he wasn't at the first enclosure, Freya loped down toward the fence as I passed by. She sank onto her front paws, her tail wagging, as if inviting me in to play.

I had to admit, she was hard to resist. If I had the keys to the gates, I'd be tempted to drop in and hang out with her a little.

"Aren't you a sweet girl," I murmured as I walked by.

Playful yelps and the sound of a man's voice greeted me as I approached the second enclosure. I shouldn't have been surprised to find Rich inside, frolicking around with Njord, but I was.

Rich called out to me and motioned me closer, so I went through the first gate and stopped. He was crouched next to Njord, petting the wolf's ears. Njord leaned in closer to his caretaker and give him a nose-kiss. The white wolf then politely sat down, waiting for more petting.

That wolf-kiss floored me. It was pretty obvious that the recognized alpha in that enclosure wasn't Njord, but Rich himself.

Had the wolves viewed Shaun as an alpha, as well? Or even all humans? If that dynamic was in place, what could have possessed them to attack Shaun?

8

"They're so fascinating, aren't they?" Veronica's voice piped up behind me.

I turned, taking in her disheveled ponytail and the dry leaf clinging to her leg. It almost looked like she'd had a fling in the woods—which seemed unlikely, given that Carson was the only one roaming around.

Ignoring my perplexed silence, Veronica brushed the leaf off and straightened her ponytail. "I managed to lose that freak," she said. Her dark eyes sought and held my gaze, almost challenging me.

Was she protesting Carson's attentions too much?

Rich, who'd been cavorting around with the two wolves that looked like litter mates, stood and made his way toward us. "I like to put my time in with them," he explained, locking the gate behind him. "They're sort of like kids—if you show them you truly like them, their loyalty knows no bounds."

Veronica scribbled something in the notebook in her hand, probably copying Rich's direct quote.

"Do you ever go into the fence?" I asked Veronica.

She shrugged. "Sure. I've gone into both enclosures. My favorite wolves are the two Rich was just playing with. They're a sister and brother—Saga and Sigurd. Siggie for short."

"Who came up with the Norse name theme?" I asked. I'd read some of *The Sagas of Icelanders* myself, back when I'd learned my dad had a few Norwegian ancestors.

Rich piped up. "That was my suggestion, and Dahlia thought it was a good one. I figured the forsaken wolves needed names that they could grow into, you know? Names that represented power and a sort of wildness."

"Makes sense." I took a step closer to him, dropping my voice. "Have you ever had any misgivings when you play with them? Especially with Njord?"

Veronica remained silent, but her pen was poised to record Rich's response.

Rich slowly shook his head. "No. I can't honestly say I have, even after… the incident with Shaun." He glanced at the wolves, who were romping with each other like excited puppies. "I don't guess I'll ever understand what happened to him. I've wondered if he was taunting the wolves somehow—maybe offering food, then holding it back. I suppose it would be possible that the wolves could kill to take the food they felt was theirs. But the moment they attacked, Shaun should have been ready with his pepper spray. I wonder if the police have found it yet."

Veronica stopped writing for a moment and pinned me with a shrewd gaze. "So, you haven't told us how *you* feel about the wolves, Belinda. Do you feel comfortable going in the enclosures?"

I answered as honestly as I could. "Not yet, but I have to admit, I'm getting there fast. The wolves have been nothing but friendly to me."

She didn't write anything down, but asked, "So would you say wolves see humans as part of their pack? Or as their prey?"

"It looks like Rich is in their pack," I said. "He actually seems to be their alpha. As for me…I don't think they see me as prey, but maybe I'm not part of the pack yet?"

Veronica scrawled my answer in silence, then capped her pen.

Rich gave me a smile. "Good answer," he said.

I glanced at my watch. "I've finished feeding the other animals, Rich. Is it okay if I head out now?"

"Of course. Just check in with Evie and let her know you're going. See you bright and early tomorrow?"

"Will do. Have a great night. You too, Veronica."

"Oh, I will," Veronica said, flashing me the kind of goofy grin that women only get when they're falling in love.

She wouldn't be falling for someone at the preserve, would she? If it was Carson, why had she been so determined to hide their relationship?

I looked over at Rich. Surely he was too old for her…and too *married*?

* * * *

I put my phone on speaker and called Mom on the way home. I had promised to check in when I'd decided whether I was going to stick with the wolf-sitting job or not. I had been delaying the call because she'd had such a tearful reaction when I told her how Shaun died.

While Mom wasn't the type to forbid me from working at the wolf preserve, she *was* the type who would read up on wolves and come up with at least twenty different methods to protect myself in case of attack. She would also search for an essential oil that had wolf-repellent qualities (maybe garlic? like vampires?), and she'd ship that down to me immediately.

Mom took her naturalistic, off-grid efforts seriously. In preparation for a nuclear war or a deadly plague—whatever was most imminent—she had even had me plant an herbal-cure flower bed on the property. So far, we had established echinacea, foxglove, poppies, lavender, mint, and calendula. If it were legal, she probably would have added marijuana and magic mushrooms to the list.

Mom picked up right after her answering machine started playing, so I had to wait for the beep. "Hi, Mom," I said.

"Belinda! Your father and I have been worried sick ever since you called last night. Have you left your job yet?"

"I've decided to stay on longer to help one of the employees out, but when the owner gets back, I'll see if I'm still needed. Is Dad around?" Although I hoped my question would distract Mom, I truly wanted to get my veterinarian dad's thoughts about wolf pack behavior and the likelihood they would have had some motive to kill and eat Shaun.

"He's over at Gerald Klein's farm—his sow's off her feed and feverish. You need him to call you?"

"Sure, that'd be great. Maybe later tonight though, since I'm heading to the Fentons' place for dinner." Ava and Adam Fenton's daughter, Margo, had been murdered last fall, and during the course of the investigation, the bereaved couple and I had become close friends.

"Oh, Ava is such a sweet lady—she just e-mailed me her recipe for raspberry-ricotta cake. Please tell her I plan to make it for the church picnic. I'm so glad you have someone looking out for you there."

Mom would never admit to it, but I was fairly certain she'd befriended Ava Fenton so quickly on her last visit simply as a means of keeping tabs on me from afar.

"I'm glad I got to know them, too," I said. Quite honestly, if something tragic happened to me in Greenwich, the only ones who would even notice right now were the Fentons and maybe Red.

As I hung up with Mom, I made a mental note to get out and try to make more friends.

The only obstacle was that I literally hated attending social functions. Stone the fifth had taken me to a polo match, and I'd stuck out like a sore thumb in my not-Greenwich-enough clothing. I'd visited some churches, but they had felt as empty as the pews inside them. I did enjoy the library, but that was only because I didn't *have* to talk to anyone there if I didn't want to.

Of course, there were plenty of people who shared my social class in Manhattan, but I needed a good reason to take the long train ride into the city on any kind of a regular basis. Maybe I could call Dietrich sometime, see if he knew of any hip parties in Brooklyn.

I chuckled at the thought. As if he would know anyone I would connect with. Dietrich was an artist (one whose artwork I couldn't appreciate), and he was still far above me socially because he'd grown up in Greenwich. We were mutual friends with Stone the fifth, and that was all.

I could get friendly with Evie, but I wasn't sure if she was friend material, especially with her penchant for suddenly dropping off the radar at work.

Nope. I'd stick with the handful of friends I already had. Besides, if anything tragic did happen to me at the wolf preserve, I knew at least one person who'd make for dead sure the wolves would never harm anyone again.

My sister.

* * * *

When I arrived at Ava Fenton's, she greeted me warmly at her door, wearing diamond chandelier earrings that would've been over the top on anyone else. Ava was a tall, bigger-boned blonde woman who wore nothing but the best designers. While she could've easily come off as queenly and imposing, her genuine acceptance of me—despite my peasant status in comparison to her wealth—was reassuring. She never spoke down to me, and I really believed she saw me as an equal.

I complimented her long navy wrap dress, and she said it was one of her favorite Ralph Laurens. Without further ado, she led me straight to her gourmet kitchen, which I'd discovered was the central hub of this home.

As I perched on a steel barstool, Ava busied herself with an appetizer dish. "How's work?" she asked.

I shared how Rich and I had stumbled onto Shaun's body. The slight tremor in Ava's hands was the only giveaway of how much my story had disturbed her.

"And you're still working there," she said. It wasn't a question.

I helped myself to the cheese and grapes she pushed my way. "Yes, but I'll get out of it as soon as I can. For now, I feel like they really need my help."

"What was the name of that wolf preserve again? Who runs it?" she asked.

"The White Pine Wolf Preserve—Dahlia White is the manager."

"That sounds familiar." Ava's brow furrowed as Adam walked into the kitchen. "Honey, do you remember hearing something about a White Pine Wolf Preserve or a Dahlia White?"

Adam, whose perpetual tan and dapper clothes always made him look like he'd participated in a regatta, stepped over and shook my hand. He plopped down next to me on a barstool and crunched into a piece of celery.

"Let's see," he said. "Remember that time a wolf escaped and showed up behind the Andersons' guesthouse, maybe a couple of years ago? Wasn't that from that place?"

Ava pointed at him and nodded. "You know, you're right." She chuckled. "Wasn't the wolf drinking from their koi pond or something?"

"It had eaten several of the fish, if I remember correctly," Adam said.

"Yes, and there was a very public feud that went on after that, between the police and that Dahlia woman," Ava added. "I think a man named Officer Jacob Hardy in particular was always writing letters to the editor and giving interviews during that time, about how the preserve didn't have adequate fencing, that kind of thing."

"Sergeant Hardy," I muttered. "But the fencing seems more than adequate now—it's eight feet high, with two locked gates and everything."

"Might've beefed up their security after that incident," Adam speculated.

"That would make sense, after all the bad publicity the place got," Ava said. She patted my arm. "How's Stone the fourth doing these days? And the younger Stone? I haven't seen them at any of their regular functions. I'm hoping Stone the fourth hasn't lapsed into his…well, his *inebriated* ways."

"Actually, I'm happy to report that he's kicked his alcoholism, from what I've heard. He's been traveling into Manhattan more often to manage his business, getting ready to hand it over to Stone the fifth."

"A wise move," Adam said. "That boy's a natural hedge fund manager. I've used him for several of my own transactions."

I hastened to explain. "Well, Stone the fifth is out of town right now. He's overseas at a retreat."

Ava gave me a knowing look. "When's he coming back, dear?"

I shifted uncomfortably on my stool. "No one really knows."

9

Later that night, after I'd taken a long soak in the bath, my dad called. He said he wasn't familiar with wolf pack behavior, but he recommended that I watch some online documentaries on the topic. Why hadn't I thought of that already?

Although it was getting late, I curled up on my bed and booted up my laptop. It didn't take long to find a documentary on YouTube about the wolves of Yellowstone Park. One particular black wolf showed extreme ingenuity in how he infiltrated an enemy pack. I watched as his entire life story unfolded, from the triumphant moment he started his own pack to the adorable litters he spawned. When the program wrapped up with the wolf's death, I started sobbing like a baby.

Of course, Jonas picked that exact moment to call.

I would have let it go to voice mail, but maybe he needed to share something urgent about his upcoming trip. After wiping my nose and eyes with a tissue, I finally picked up.

"Yes? Hi!" I tried to sound upbeat.

"Belinda? You okay? You sound like something's wrong."

So much for that. There was no reason to hide my stupid sob fest from Jonas; besides, I didn't want him worrying about me. "Yeah, I was just watching this video about a wolf and he was so smart and he had the cutest litters of pups, but then he died."

Jonas seemed to make sense of my disjointed explanation. "Sad nature show—gotcha. Are you really getting attached to those wolves?"

"I don't know. I can't shake the impression that they're actually welcoming and not truly dangerous, no matter what happened with Shaun. There's this one scarred-up wolf, Freya, and she seems determined to be my friend."

"Maybe she is, and maybe those wolves do seem welcoming, but one thing I've learned being a dairy farmer is that even the calmest-tempered animals can fool you. One of my sweetest Jersey cows nearly stomped me to death when I tried to bring her calf inside last winter. And unlike cows, remember that wolves are wild."

Why was it Jonas and Katrina were nearly always on the same page?

By the time I hung up with Jonas, I was certain of two things. The first was that the man could read me like a book, and I wasn't sure if that was a good or a bad thing. The second was that I should continue to proceed cautiously in the wolf enclosures, even when the animals seemed friendly.

I didn't want to let my guard down just because of some moving wolf documentary and become victim number two.

* * * *

It was so warm the next day, I was able to wear short sleeves and roll down Bluebell's window for some fresh air. The April weather had certainly been a bit schizophrenic, but I was thankful for the sun.

When I reached the driveway to the preserve, I had to dodge parked vehicles emblazoned with various news station logos. Reporters streamed up the drive, eager to get the scoop. As I pulled up behind the mid-drive gate, several cameramen seemed to be recording footage of the visitors' center.

I jumped out and crept between them until I could try the gate. It was locked.

How was I supposed to get to work? My overactive gamer imagination pictured the reporters and cameramen morphing into zombies, then streaming like a flood over the top of my car, banging on my windows until they broke, pulling me from behind the wheel...

I hurled myself back into Bluebell and frantically called Evie. "I'm outside the gate and I can't get in!"

Evie didn't seem too concerned. "Righty-o. I'll head down and open it, then you can drive in."

"But the reporters are everywhere! I don't know how I'll get around them!"

"No worries, love. I'll shoo them off."

True to her word, Evie zipped down the drive in a golf cart. I hadn't seen the green cart before, but it was quite striking, with a gray wolf's head stenciled on both sides.

I'd rolled my windows up, leaving only the slightest crack, but Evie's British accent rang out loud and clear as she unlocked the gate. "Fall back, you tossers, so things don't get argy-bargy!"

The reporters, probably uncertain what language Evie was speaking, began to shuffle out of my way as I edged Bluebell forward. Evie slammed the gate shut behind my Volvo and locked it again, throwing out an enigmatic "Cheers!" to the annoying crowd.

After parking, I caught up to Evie, who had turned off the golf cart and was striding toward the visitors' center.

"So the news broke?" I asked.

She nodded. "Yes, but thankfully Dahlia got home last night. She's actually inside—I'm catching her up on things."

Evie pushed open the barn door and sure enough, Dahlia had sunk into a chair next to the cash register. Dark circles stood out under her eyes, and her light, frizzy hair looked like she hadn't even run a comb through it. I suspected this wasn't the first day she'd worn her rumpled outfit.

Evie, who had also dressed more casually than usual, walked past me. She wordlessly took a notebook from Dahlia and sat down next to her.

Dahlia's voice was shaky. "Belinda, I hope this hasn't been too horrible for you. I'm so pleased you didn't jump ship. You've certainly lived up to your reputation as a fearless pet-sitter."

She seemed so genuinely pleased to have me around, I couldn't think of any good way to find out if she was actually going to start helping Rich, as she'd planned to do before her trip.

"I'm doing okay," I said. "Rich has helped me so much. He's amazing with the wolves."

"Mm-hmm," Dahlia said, glancing at the paper Evie had handed her. "I really need to get caught up, but be sure to check in with me later today, okay?"

"Oh, of course. I'm glad you're back."

As I went into the kitchen to grab my green vest, I overheard Dahlia lamenting how she'd probably have to talk to the media. "Maybe you could speak for me, Evie?"

"No, I can't do that." Evie's voice was unusually abrupt.

Dahlia sighed. "If Sergeant Hardy didn't have it out for me, the press wouldn't even know. We could still be giving tours."

"He's put off telling the media as long as he could, so you had time to return," Evie said. "And it's not exactly the kind of death you can cover up, then carry on as you were before."

I quietly opened the side door and walked outside. It was clear that Dahlia would be distraught for a while, at least until the media coverage of Shaun's death subsided. I doubted she was going to be able to help Rich when she would have a huge struggle just making the preserve look safe for tourists.

After taking quick glances into the red building and around the smaller animal fences, I realized Rich must have already gone out to the wolf enclosures. He had probably loaded the meats while I was delayed by the front gate.

I decided to take the long way around, a reversal of our usual route. I needed to ask myself some serious questions, like whether I was truly prepared to stay for the duration of my contract if Dahlia didn't step up to the plate to help Rich. She had the most endearing way of truly believing in my exotic pet-sitting abilities, and I hated to disillusion her by leaving both her and Rich in the lurch.

The sunshine was restorative, as were the calming sounds of spring birds and the burbling creek. I stopped for a moment and closed my eyes, surprised to find I was wishing myself back home to Larches Corner.

I let my mind drift. My ideal day at home would start with one of my sister's cinnamon rolls and a cup of coffee from The Coffee Shoppe downtown—I'd choose the flavor of the day, since I rarely had the same coffee drink twice. Then I'd swing by Jonas's place to talk with him and his mom about anything from flowers to philosophy to the actual ages of movie stars. Then I'd ramble home through my parents' woods, maybe take the four-wheeler out for a spin. After some of my homemade lasagna (I was a better cook than my mom), we'd relax on the porch awhile. The peachy sunset would fade into a velvety navy sky spangled with stars, and I'd fall asleep with my window open, listening to the peepers outside.

Something interrupted my blissful musings of home—a prolonged shout. More like a scream?

I froze in place, waiting to see if I'd somehow imagined the sound.

10

Another screech followed, and I raced toward it. The second wolf enclosure came into view as I topped a little hill. Carson staggered out of the second gate, holding his hand and screaming.

Njord darted away from the fence line, like a guilty child caught in the act. The other wolves weren't around.

Carson stumbled toward me. Blood was dripping from his hand, and his face had paled to a deathly white.

I steeled myself and sprang into my efficient caregiver mode—something I'd perfected when accompanying my dad to his farm house calls. Quite a few times, I'd wound up murmuring comforting words to the farmers or pitching in to help my dad with the tasks at hand—no matter how stomach-turning they turned out to be.

"Hang on," I said, hoping Carson wasn't going into shock. I whipped off my green vest and looked at his bleeding hand. One finger had obviously been gnawed on, and there were a few deeper gashes on it, as well. I wrapped the finger thoroughly, then swathed the rest of his hand with the remaining fabric.

"I'm going to get you back where they can help you," I said. "Hold on to me."

Carson listlessly allowed me to drape his uninjured arm around my neck, then we slowly staggered toward the visitors' center. I wished I had a golf cart, because I surely didn't care if I disturbed the wolves at this point.

"How'd this happen?" I probed.

"I didn't know they were so hungry," Carson said, his eyes wide behind his glasses. "I just wanted to pet them, so I let myself into the first gate, then tried to pet him through the fencing." He let out a yelp as I stumbled over a rock in the path. "Can't…remember anything else. Gah! It's so freaking painful!"

He held his injured hand tightly to his chest, like he feared it would fall off. If I wasn't so concerned, I would have had to laugh at the nearly theatrical performance the reserved preppie had brought to the table.

As we passed by the first wolf enclosure, it dawned on me that Rich was nowhere in sight. I couldn't imagine what else he would be doing, if he wasn't with the wolves or the smaller animals. Maybe he didn't come in this morning for some reason and Evie had forgotten to tell me? That would mean I'd have to feed and water both packs today. My breathing quickened, and I had to slow to refocus on the task at hand. I adjusted Carson's arm, which was slipping from my shoulder, and tried to lead him along more quickly.

By the time we saw the visitors' center, Carson was moaning loudly. I figured it was for Veronica's benefit, but she didn't seem to be around, either.

"We need some help here!" I shouted, hoping someone would aid me with my human burden. Carson's arm hung like deadweight over my shoulder, and he leaned against me heavily.

Evie rushed out. To her credit, she didn't even gasp when she saw the bloody vest. I quickly explained what had happened.

"I'll call an ambulance," she said, extracting her phone from her pocket. "You two go inside with Dahlia and sit down."

I gladly complied. Weary of the weight, I gently removed Carson's arm from my neck, then walked him inside and toward an empty chair.

As he sank into it, his mother ran out of the kitchen, which inspired a fresh outburst of moaning.

"Oh, my poor boy! What's happened?"

"One of your wolf babies decided to chew on my hand," he wailed.

I couldn't really stand to watch more. Although I felt terrible for Carson, he had morphed into some kind of attention hog.

"I'll check to see how things are coming with the ambulance," I said.

Dahlia seemed too distracted to register my words. She stooped in front of Carson, her hands wrapped around his good hand. Her skin had blanched to white, and when she swayed on her feet, I rushed to wrap an arm around her. I led her to the closest chair and told her to put her head in her lap. I'd seen people pass out in my dad's vet office before, and Dahlia was definitely teetering on that brink.

Evie returned and reported, "They should be here in a couple of minutes." She gave Dahlia a rueful look. "I also called the police, because Sergeant Hardy told me I had to if the wolves exhibited any other violent behavior."

Dahlia nodded absently, giving further proof of her total preoccupation with Carson. She kept stealing occasional glances at her son's bloody vest-bandage, but each time, she closed her eyes as if unable to cope.

Carson seemed to have tired of moaning. Instead, he was slumping lower and lower into his chair, as if melting into the floor.

When the ambulance roared up with sirens blazing, Evie and I went out to meet it. A police car pulled up soon after, and Sergeant Hardy practically leaped out.

Evie turned to me, whispering loudly. "You deal with him," she instructed. "I'll deal with the ambulance."

I didn't know what I'd done to earn the task of defusing the obviously outraged sergeant, but I was determined to pull my own weight around here now that everything had hit the fan.

Sergeant Hardy looked like he was about to follow Evie as she led the paramedics inside, but I held up my palm to stop him. "I can tell you what you need to know," I said. "I was the first one to see Carson White after his attack today."

The tall sergeant looked down, as if seeing me for the first time. I was five-foot-four, but I felt only five feet tall next to the brawny man.

"Belinda Blake, correct?"

"Yes, that's right. Evie asked me to fill you in."

The sergeant took out his notepad. "So, what happened?"

"I found Carson just outside the second wolf enclosure, and his hand was dripping blood. From what I could tell, one of his fingers had been chewed on, and there were gashes on his hand. I wrapped his finger and walked him back to the visitors' center, where Evie called the ambulance."

"What was he doing with the wolves? Anything unusual?"

"It didn't sound like he'd done anything out of the ordinary. He just said he had tried to pet the wolves through the fencing." I paused. "Although he did mention that he was surprised the wolves were hungry."

I was startled when the sergeant hastily snaked his hand to my elbow and steered me sideways—until I followed his line of sight and saw paramedics carrying Carson's stretcher through the visitors' center door. The poor, injured drama king had resorted to spurts of bawling at this point, and as he turned his completely un-reddened face to me, I felt certain he was shedding crocodile tears. Evie trailed after the paramedics, accompanying them to the ambulance, and I wondered where Dahlia was.

As the ambulance drove away, Evie told us that the paramedics had instructed Dahlia to rest at her house, given her inability to deal with her son's bleeding. They had reassured her that Carson would be okay.

"I'm going to go over and check on Dahlia," Evie said. "Are you two wrapping things up here, or do you need anything further?"

Sergeant Hardy frowned. "Actually, I'm afraid we're far from wrapping up. I'll need to examine the wolf enclosure where this happened. Also, the preserve is going to be closed indefinitely until we square things away."

Evie's eyes widened, but the sergeant's firm tone made it clear he wasn't going to brook any argument. She nodded briskly. "Certainly. I will let Dahlia know, and I'll cancel tours for the next few weeks. Belinda, could you gather up my tour lists while I get Dahlia settled? And Sergeant Hardy, can you find your own way to the wolf enclosures?"

Sergeant Hardy nodded, then motioned to his partner, who had been sitting in the police car.

"You might also want to compose a statement for the reporters," the sergeant said. "They were filming the ambulance and our car as we drove in. Those sharks know there's literal blood in the water now."

Evie paled, giving the sergeant a beseeching look. "I…I can't. Dahlia will have to say something, and she's in no shape… How do you recommend we deal with this?"

The sergeant's face hardened. "There's no way to spin a situation like this, where one man is dead and another has been mauled. Now that I think about it, maybe your best plan would be to remain silent."

I hardly thought that was a good course of action, when Dahlia's entire business was riding on her ability to convince tour groups they wanted to come here, but then again, the sergeant had a point. There was absolutely no way to spin wolf attacks at a wolf preserve.

Sergeant Hardy stalked off, his partner on his heels.

"I guess that's that, then." Evie's long arms went slack by her side and her steps were heavy as she walked into the darkened gift shop.

I followed, scrambling to think of a way to lift her spirits. "If you really wanted someone to give a statement to the reporters, I could do it," I offered.

She turned and gave me a wan smile. "That is kind of you, Belinda, but it's too late for statements, I suppose." She strode into the kitchen and poured fresh water into the electric teakettle.

I reflected a moment on her strangely adamant refusal to offer a statement on behalf of the preserve. Wasn't that part of her job?

I stepped closer. "Excuse me if I'm being too bold, but I was surprised you didn't want to speak to the reporters. You're so outgoing, and you certainly know the ins and outs of this place. Besides, if you can handle irritated tourists, the press can't be very different."

Evie dropped two English breakfast tea bags into mugs, but her lips thinned into a tight line.

"I mean it's okay," I rambled on. "You're just such an enthusiastic person. At this point, I'm sure you'd do a much better job of things than Dahlia."

She stared at the counter, swirling one of the tea bags in the water. "I'm glad you think so. I don't feel enthusiastic much of the time." She raised her head and gave me a fleeting look.

I caught my breath as I recognized something in her glance.

The brown wolf, Freya, had shot me the same kind of wounded, overly hopeful look—one that said she'd been hurt so deeply, she didn't even know how to trust anymore.

Who had crushed Evie's spirit like this? Was it the same person she'd been hiding out from?

As Evie picked up one of the mugs and headed for the side door, I realized she'd brewed the second cup for Dahlia and was probably taking it to her.

Katrina had often told us, "You have to build a supportive environment in order for someone to start to heal." With those words in mind, I shoved the door open for Evie, then said, "Hey, would you want to head somewhere for lunch tomorrow? There are some great places nearby, and it would give us a break from the daily grind—such as it is."

She wrapped both hands around the mug. "I would enjoy that," she said. "Oh, and those tour lists should be behind the front desk, if you don't mind getting those together for me. I'll need to start calling everyone when I return."

"Sure. I'll stack them on your desk before I head out," I said.

I pulled the door closed behind her, happy I'd taken the initiative and asked her to lunch. With the combination of her furtive behavior and her injured look, I knew there was something weighing on her.

And it was entirely possible that it was connected to Shaun's death.

11

It took longer than I'd planned to go through Evie's tour lists. Apparently, she was the kind of person who had her own system that appeared messy to everyone else but her. Tour groups were listed on random pieces of paper, and I had to do some digging to match phone numbers with contact names. I had just finished compiling a master list for Evie when she returned.

She looked over what I had done. "That's simply brilliant," she said. "I can't thank you enough for helping me so much today. Dahlia is basically off her head, she's so worried about Carson. She wants to be with him, but doesn't feel strong enough, so I suggested we call someone who could go to the hospital and stay with him. She finally let me call Carson's grandpa—Dennis Arden—so he's heading over there now and can give us updates."

"Sounds like a good plan."

Evie tugged at a dangling silver earring. "I hate to ask you for anything else, but would you mind going out and making sure the police found the right enclosure? I would do it myself, but I need to start calling people."

"No problem," I said, jumping on the opportunity to get a little fresh air.

I left Evie to make her customer calls and strode outside. The baby blue sky, full of fluffy clouds, seemed completely incongruous with the wolf attack that had occurred today.

Once again, I was struck by the fact that Rich hadn't showed up, even with all the tumult at the visitors' center. Was he even here today? Would I have to feed the wolves alone? Surely Evie would have told me if something had come up for him.

And then there was Veronica. Was she going to stay on any regular schedule, now that she wasn't leading tours? Today's turn of events would definitely play into her master's thesis nicely. Would she care that Carson had been injured, or would she laugh?

I reached the first enclosure and found the sergeant's partner examining part of the fence. "This isn't the right enclosure," I said. "You want the one with the white wolf."

He nodded. "We weren't sure, so we checked this one first, but didn't find any signs of struggle or blood. The sergeant just headed over to the other enclosure."

"Okay. Thanks for letting me know." I picked up my pace and was jogging by the time I reached Njord's enclosure, anxious to see if the wolves were acting strangely.

What I saw there made me stop in my tracks.

Almost in slow motion, I watched as Sergeant Hardy put his hand on his gun and slipped it out. He aimed toward the gate, and I held my breath so I wouldn't make a sound and startle him. My eyes flew to the wolves, but I only saw Njord.

And once again, the white wolf was standing over a body.

I blinked, hoping I was just seeing things, but the body was still there. I wasn't able to tell who it was, or if the person was still alive. Was the sergeant going to shoot Njord right here and now?

One shot rang out, but all it did was blow the lock on the first gate. Njord tore off, heading deeper into the wooded section of the enclosure. Sergeant Hardy repeated the process with the other lock, then stepped into the second gate.

The sergeant's partner raced toward him, stopping behind the second gate.

"I didn't have time to get the key, but I've called for backup," Sergeant Hardy said, edging toward the body. "Cover me, but block the gate in case the wolves try to escape."

As the sergeant crouched next to the body, he felt for a pulse. I still couldn't make out the person's face.

He turned and shook his head. "The victim is deceased," he said. "Radio it in."

I took a deep breath and stepped closer to the first gate. None of the wolves were in sight.

"Who is it?" I asked. "Dahlia and Evie will need to know."

Sergeant Hardy shifted so I could see better.

Suddenly, I wished he hadn't.

The kind, fatherly face of Rich O'Brien stared at the ground with lifeless eyes.

I grabbed at the gate for support, unable to stand. Just yesterday, Rich had been playing with these very wolves. This was some kind of mistake.

I forced myself to look closer. There wasn't a bit of blood on Rich. In fact, from where I stood, his body looked like it was in pristine condition.

"You think this was a wolf attack?" I asked.

Sergeant Hardy gave me a puzzled look. "There are no visible injuries."

The other officer stopped talking on his radio and turned to me, giving me a once-over. "Ma'am, are you able to return to the visitors' center and alert them to this? Or do you need me to accompany you?"

I was probably paler than pale and my limbs felt wobbly, but I knew what I had to do. "No, please stay and get Rich out of there. But thank you."

I propelled myself into motion and didn't slow as I passed the first enclosure. Veronica was pacing outside the visitors' center, and she actually looked worried.

"Evie told me what happened to Carson," she said. "I feel bad. Once I saw Carson heading into the woods this morning, I stayed back and restacked the bags of chicken feed. I couldn't risk having him leech onto me again, because I get next to no research done when he's around."

I understood how frustrating it must be for her, but I surely didn't have time to linger for a chat. "Is Evie still inside?"

Veronica nodded, falling silent.

I walked toward the door, but stopped when I caught a movement out of the corner of my eye. I whipped around and focused on a bulky man standing at the edge of the parking lot. He looked directly at me, then dodged into the woods.

Veronica stared in the same direction. She gave me a curious look. "Who was that?"

"Probably a reporter," I said, telling myself that was the most likely explanation.

But the man hadn't been carrying a camera.

And the unguarded look on his face had been one of sheer animosity.

* * * *

Veronica stayed outside the visitors' center so she could let us know if the man returned. I went inside and found Evie in the kitchen, munching half-heartedly on a scone. I hated to drop the news of another death on her, but she seemed to be more capable of handling it than Dahlia at this point.

"Brace yourself," I said.

She put down the scone and dusted crumbs off her hands. "Yes?"

"There's been another death."

Evie's eyebrows furrowed in an attempt to process the news, but she didn't respond. Maybe I'd miscalculated her ability to deal with ghastly situations right now.

I patted her shoulder, hoping to jolt her from her apparent shock. Softening my tone, I said, "I hate to tell you, but Rich has died, in Njord's enclosure. The police are out there now. We'll probably need to find something to help them secure the gates, since they had to shoot the locks off to check on him."

Evie picked up her cup of tea, absently took a sip, then held it aloft as if unable to think what to do next.

I tried to be patient, but Evie needed to snap back to reality so we could clean up this mess. "Evie, this is serious. We need to help the cops with things, and we're going to have to tell Dahlia what's happened. But maybe not just yet, if she's still resting at her house. In fact, we won't worry about Dahlia. We can just ask Sergeant Hardy what he needs from us, okay?"

Her face crumpled. "But...Rich? How? Why?"

Those were the right questions. Why would the wolves have killed Rich, their recognized human alpha? Besides, it hadn't looked like they'd killed him at all. So how did he wind up dead in the wolf enclosure?

Things didn't add up.

* * * *

By the time Evie, Veronica, and I had scrounged up enough rope to temporarily hold the gates, more police vehicles had arrived. Officers swarmed into the woods, toting forensic equipment. I had actually welcomed Veronica's help, because Evie was far from her generally efficient self.

Sergeant Hardy and his partner walked briskly past the others to meet us in front of the visitors' center. The steely glint in Sergeant Hardy's eyes said he was finished playing around.

Evie shook her head, extending the rope toward the sergeant. "I just can't believe—"

He cut her off. "I'm going to find out which wolves are killing people, and I'm going to put them down myself."

Well. That certainly didn't seem too PETA-friendly, but I figured that was protocol when there was a rash of killings by wild animals, even animals in a secure enclosure. I tried to recall what had happened years ago when a gorilla attacked a toddler in a zoo. I was pretty certain they'd killed the gorilla.

Sergeant Hardy handed the proffered rope back to Evie. "We've already secured the gates with new locks. Here's the key, Ms. Grady." He gingerly handed it to her, as if aware of her state of shock. "And where is Ms. White?"

Evie looked like a deer in the headlights, and I felt truly sorry for her. This entire situation was so far beyond the bounds of what she was supposed to be handling, and Dahlia had been practically AWOL since she got home.

Evie motioned toward the white farmhouse. "The last I checked, she was resting. I haven't told her about Rich's death yet."

Sergeant Hardy's face was unyielding. "She needs to know about it."

Evie's face blanched. It was clear that she didn't want to hear details of what had happened to Rich, much less report them to Dahlia.

One of the officers and Veronica both approached Sergeant Hardy at the same time. The sergeant's gaze first traveled to Veronica, lingering there just a second too long. I caught a flicker of unveiled softness in his eyes. This girl really made an impression on men, it seemed.

Veronica placed a hand on Sergeant Hardy's arm. "Is there anything I can do to help?" she asked, giving him a little nudge.

I couldn't believe she was being so bold, but no one else seemed to notice it. The officer hung back at a respectful distance until Sergeant Hardy had gently dismissed Veronica by telling her he'd talk to her later.

Once the officer had finished talking, I stepped closer to Sergeant Hardy. "I'll let Dahlia know what's happened. I wanted to check and see how Carson was doing, anyway."

Evie shot me a grateful look.

I hesitated, wishing I could tell Sergeant Hardy about the strange man in the parking lot, but that might bump Evie's slowly recovering equilibrium. I ambled away, figuring I could catch up with the sergeant a little later. His cleanup crew didn't seem to be going anywhere fast.

Besides, the real reason I'd volunteered to talk to Dahlia was because I needed to find out if she had anyone else who could step in to feed the wolves. I surely wasn't going to do it.

12

As I walked over to the white house, I pondered the dubious nature of Veronica's claim that she'd been moving chicken feed when Carson was yelling for help this morning. I didn't know if Veronica had ever fed the chickens, but it didn't seem to be the kind of chore that was up her alley.

Unable to locate a doorbell, I rapped on the cherry-red front door. A couple of moments passed, and I was just getting ready to ring again when I heard Dahlia shout, "I'm coming!"

She must have scrambled down the stairs, because she was out of breath when she cracked the door and peered out into the sunlight. "Belinda?"

"Hi, Dahlia, do you mind if I come in?"

"Of course not. Come inside." She motioned me into the cool interior of the hallway. "What's going on?"

"First, I wondered how Carson is doing," I asked, hoping to ease into the real reason for my visit.

"His grandfather just called." She twisted a tissue in her hands. "He said Carson's fingers are all intact and nothing was severed. Everything should heal in a few weeks."

"That was a close call, though. His hand was really messed up." It seemed that Dahlia could at least acknowledge that her wolves were dangerous.

"Yes," Dahlia murmured.

Maybe what I said next would force her to acknowledge the wolves' deadly tendencies. "Something else has happened. Sergeant Hardy found Rich in Njord's enclosure, and I hate to say it, but Rich is dead."

I watched her response closely. She clasped her hands to her heart and stared. "What?! No!"

She seemed genuinely upset, so I rushed to smooth things as best I could. "Sergeant Hardy said we needed to be prepared for the press coverage, so you might need to talk with Evie about how to present the story."

"I can't possibly talk to the reporters." Dahlia ran a hand through her unkempt hair.

"Evie's certainly not in any shape to do it, either," I said. "But if you two talk it out, maybe you can figure out an angle that will somehow keep your place in business."

Dahlia sank into an antique chair. "That's the rub, isn't it? No one's going to want to book tours here now. So what will happen to the wolves?"

At least she seemed concerned about the plight of her animals.

I shrugged. "I don't know." Hesitating a moment, I decided to plunge ahead with my real question. "Um…speaking of the wolves, I hate to ask, but do you have anyone else who knows how Rich feeds them? I only did the water, and to be truthful, right now I'd feel really uncomfortable going back into their enclosures."

Dahlia looked thoughtful. "Well, Veronica has fed them, but she's so tiny…she couldn't fight them off."

She failed to mention that Shaun had been far from small, and he hadn't been able to fight them off. Besides, what was I, a looming giant? Far from it.

She pulled her cell phone from her shirt pocket and scrolled down the list, thinking out loud. "Evie can't do it; she's afraid of the wolves. And Carson has always wanted to feed them, but I haven't felt he was ready, and now…"

She sniffed and untwisted her tissue to wipe her tears. Suddenly, her finger stopped on a contact name. "Marco! I'll call him. He's filled in for Rich before. Maybe you could help him, just with the water?"

There it was, the question I'd been dreading. Would I risk life and limb to enter the enclosures again? This job certainly wasn't worth it, no matter how well it paid.

"I'll think about it," I said.

She nodded hopefully. "I'll call Marco. Then I'll talk to Evie." She pushed a button and put her phone to her ear, so I waved and headed out.

Back in the sunshine, I inhaled the sweet smell of hyacinths lining Dahlia's walkway. I wished I could head home and recuperate from seeing Rich's lifeless body, but I would probably have to take care of all the smaller animals before I left. It was anyone's guess if Veronica had actually fed the chickens after she shifted their feed around.

In one final act of kindness, Rich must have fed the wolves before his death, since I'd spotted empty buckets in the wheelbarrow he'd left just outside the gate. As I mulled over the logistics of that setup, I frowned. It wasn't like Rich to abandon his wheelbarrow only to reenter the enclosure. Had he unlocked the gates just to give the wolves a final petting?

Regardless of how Rich's last moments had played out, it was agonizing to imagine how his family was going to react to the news of his death. His daughter was just on the brink of getting married. I couldn't help but imagine myself in her shoes. Although my dad had seen some close calls as a vet, if he had been killed in some kind of wolf attack…well, I knew what my reaction would be.

It would be about the same as Sergeant Hardy's—I'd want those monsters put down.

* * * *

Once my small-animal chores were finished, I checked in with Evie. After a lot of back-and-forth, she had managed to talk Dahlia into giving a statement this evening to the reporters who were still lined up outside the gate. The intrepid journalists had certainly enjoyed front row seats for the parade of ambulances and police cars today, and it was a given that the White Pine Wolf Preserve was going to dominate the local front-page news this week. I wondered if the bulky man who had scrambled into the woods would be present at the press briefing.

Evie said Dahlia wasn't going to answer specific questions—she would just say the police were working on things and the preserve would be closed for a few weeks. Overall, she would attempt to give the impression that things were well under control, which, of course, they weren't.

I doubted that Dahlia's statement would stave off the ravening media hordes for long, but it was worth a shot.

"Marco will be here tomorrow to help you with the wolves," Evie said. "Should we still plan on lunch?"

I figured she was asking me, in a roundabout way, if I was ever going to show up again.

Since Marco was coming in tomorrow, I figured I'd be safe enough to stick with the job for now. Besides, I could always call if I made some kind of last-minute decision to quit. "Let's do that. There's a taco place I've been dying to try and it seems reasonably priced."

Evie gave a relieved nod. "See you tomorrow."

Once I stepped outside, I allowed myself a brief dip in a mental pool of despondency. It was surreal that I would never again chat with Rich at the end of a workday at White Pine.

As I slid into Bluebell's driver's seat, my sadness morphed into an unwillingness to face the news reporters who were gathered on the driveway. I delayed my exit, calling Katrina instead.

My sister picked up on the first ring, a sure sign she was bored out of her mind. "Tell me you're not in trouble, because I don't have the energy to rescue you."

I laughed. "Is that how you think of me? Your little sis who's always in trouble?"

"Pretty much," she said.

I had to admit, her view wasn't actually that far off. "How's little Jasper?"

"Kicking like he wants to get out. I wish he'd just get on with it."

"You're not due for a few weeks. Give him time to incubate in there."

"Easy to say, hard to do. Anyway, Mom's planning to come as soon as I start having serious contractions." Katrina sighed. "I'm not sure if that makes me feel better or worse. I hope she doesn't try to give me herbal vitamins or oils that'll help with labor. Tyler won't hear of anything that's not on our birth plan."

Katrina's husband, Tyler, happened to be an obstetrician, and he had probably run into more than his share of my mom's naturalistic remedies during this pregnancy.

"I'll bet." I sounded morose, even to myself.

Katrina's voice sharpened. "What's up? Are you at work?"

"I'm about to head home." I took a deep breath. "Kat, there's been another death in that same wolf enclosure. But this one wasn't a mauling, like the other. In fact, he didn't seem to have a scratch on him."

"Then how did it happen?"

That was the question that was tormenting me. If the wolves hadn't killed Rich—which seemed impossible without leaving marks on his body—then what had killed him? Natural causes didn't seem to fit at his age.

"I don't know."

A protective edge crept into her voice. "It's not safe there anymore. You don't have to stay."

I knew that, but the more I pictured Njord in that enclosure, standing over Rich's body, the more I was convinced that something was very off about the whole scenario. Rich had said he'd been there at Njord's birth. It seemed extremely dubious that a wolf would turn on someone who'd been in his life from day one. More than that, it was the *way* Njord had been standing next to Rich's body. He'd never entertained the slightest notion about laying a tooth on the man, I was certain.

My grip tightened on the phone. "You remember with those murders last year, how I knew something wasn't right? How I suspected it was a frame job?"

"Yes, but what does that have to do with anything?"

"This feels the same."

Katrina groaned. "But it's the wolves that have been killing people. They're the murderers, BB."

I turned the key in the ignition. "That's the thing. It feels like—I know this sounds impossible—but I think someone's framing the wolves."

13

A woman stood on my carriage house doorstep as I pulled into my roundabout drive. She had a medium-length auburn shag and she wore a flowered skirt and high wedge sandals. She held some kind of covered plate in her hands.

I opened my car door and walked her way, certain she must be lost. "Hello. Were you looking for someone?"

She nodded, batting her long eyelashes. "Belinda Blake. Are you her?"

Her words dripped with a honeyed Southern accent. Why on earth was this stranger looking for me?

"Yes, I'm Belinda," I said hesitantly. "And you are?"

She stepped down next to me, beaming a wide smile. "I'm Susan Snodgrass. Red told me about you, and I wanted to bring you a little something, by way of introduction."

"And how do you know Red?" I asked.

"We're dating," she said, a blush creeping into her cheeks.

I relaxed, giving her an unabashed grin. "Come on in. Any friend of Red's is a friend of mine."

After unlocking my door, I led her into my living room. She started to unbuckle her sandal straps. "No need to take your shoes off," I said. I raised the blinds on my back windows to let in more light, then motioned to my couch. "Please, have a seat."

She sat down demurely, setting the plate on the coffee table. "I thought you might enjoy some of my homemade lemon pound cake."

My mouth started watering. "I'm sure I will. I'm no baker, but my sister is, and fresh-baked goods are my Achilles' heel. Do you live in Greenwich?"

"I'm in Stamford, actually. I own a bakery—that's how I met Red. He has a serious sweet tooth."

"He likes his bear claws," I joked.

"Oh, honey, yes. I think he's addicted to my éclairs." She stretched her tan legs and smiled. "He's mentioned you quite a bit. I think he worries about you. He said you're working over at that wolf preserve? I saw the news about that young man's death. I hope you're not working directly with those wolves?"

Something about Susan's warm hazel eyes made me want to open up. "I am, actually. But so far, I've never been alone in their enclosures." I hesitated, unsure if I should break the news of Rich's death. I decided that would only worry everyone more. "It's stressful," I said finally.

Susan placed a hand on my own. "Listen, if you need to decompress, Red and I would be happy to take you to the beach, out shopping...you name it. I know you're all alone in town, and my heart goes out to single girls trying to make ends meet on their own. Why, shoot, I am one!"

We laughed together, and it was just the catharsis I needed. While I loved Ava and Adam Fenton, Susan was closer to my age, and I already felt like I'd known her for years. Red had chosen a winner.

Susan shared that she'd moved to Stamford to stay with her ailing grandmother, who'd died last year. She'd decided to take over her grandmother's restaurant and turn it into a French bakery called The Apricot Macaron, and it had grown into a lucrative business. I smiled as she enunciated the name—she pronounced *apricot* with a long "a," like "ape-ri-cot."

Her hands, decorated with gold rings on every other finger, fluttered as she spoke. "As a matter of fact, I saw the picture in the paper of the woman who owns the wolf preserve, and I'm certain she visited my bakery not too long ago. She got into a heated discussion with some man."

My interest was piqued. "What did he look like?"

"He had gray hair. Average height. He ate a huge croissant, I remember."

"Did you hear what they were arguing about?"

"Something about money was all I overheard. It got busy soon after they started arguing. I almost thought I was going to have to ask them to leave."

Did this argument play into the deaths on the preserve? Rich had gray hair, as did Dennis Arden. Was it possible she'd met with one of them to discuss financial issues, then had a serious disagreement?

Susan glanced at her monogrammed bracelet watch and gasped. "Oh, good gracious, I have to get going. I was supposed to meet up with Red ten minutes ago. But I've just had the best time with you. Now, you tell me what you think of that pound cake—I use extra lemon, so there's a tangy bite to it."

I walked her to the door. "I know I'll love it. You two have a wonderful date. I'm sure I'll drop by your bakery sometime."

"You do that."

After she waved good-bye, I headed inside to shower and change. I needed to go shopping for meal supplies, since Jonas would be over tomorrow.

I found myself singing at the top of my lungs as I conditioned my wet curls. I hated that I was feeling excited about Jonas's visit in the face of the tragic deaths at the wolf preserve, but his presence would be like a shelter from the storm.

* * * *

After a more-than-successful shopping expedition, which I returned from with enough food to feed an army, as well as an embroidered peasant blouse I hadn't been able to resist, I settled down to a meal of leftovers. I was thoroughly engrossed in the final chapters of *The Great Gatsby* when my cell phone rang.

Dahlia was on the other end. "We gave a statement, but I'm fairly certain reporters will be crawling around in the morning to get video footage. Please don't talk to them."

"Don't worry, I wouldn't think of it," I said. "How's Carson?"

"He's back home. Veronica brought him some Chinese food tonight, which was sweet."

Sweet, indeed. What game was Veronica playing, first trash-talking Carson behind his back and then catering to him?

"Are you...coming in tomorrow?" Dahlia asked. "I know Rich was happy with your work—he told me you were an excellent employee. Marco is comfortable with feeding the wolves, so you wouldn't have any new duties."

I realized she was attempting to cajole me into it. Had Rich *really* told her I was doing good work? I doubted he had even talked to her much, given his clear conviction that she didn't really care for the wolves.

It didn't matter if she was stretching the truth, though. I had already decided to stick with my job for the duration of the contract, in hopes of uncovering something that would shine a light on what had really happened to Shaun and Rich.

"You can count on me," I said.

* * * *

A nightmare roused me somewhere around four in the morning, and I sat straight up, gasping for breath.

In my dream, I had watched as dirt-encrusted fingers poked through the ground inside Njord's enclosure. Instinctively, I realized they were Rich's hands. The filthy hands grew larger and larger, grasping for me, trying to pull me back into the depths with them.

It wasn't the first time I'd had a dream like this—one that felt like an ominous portent. A few times, my most memorable dreams had eventually played out in ways I couldn't have seen coming. I was left wondering why on earth I'd been privy to them when I was powerless to change the natural course of events.

But this dream was no prophecy. Rich was already dead. There was nothing I could do to help him now, to free him from the grave.

Between the nightmare and my underlying excitement over Jonas's visit, I was too wired to go back to sleep. Reluctantly, I rolled out of bed, shrugged into a sweater to ward off the chill in the house, and flipped on my game system. It was as good a time as any to get caught up on gaming—and I couldn't think of a faster way to take my mind off one of the most dangerous pet-sitting jobs I'd ever accepted.

14

The alarm sounded far too early. I stumbled into the bathroom and splashed my face repeatedly with warm water in an attempt to force my tired eyes open.

Once I'd vigorously patted dry with a towel, I headed into the kitchen and brewed a cup of coffee. Leaning against the counter, I helped myself to two pieces of Susan's rapturous lemon cake, then washed that down with two cups of black coffee. I shoved food in a lunch bag, threw on my work clothes, and trudged out to Bluebell.

Dew glistened on spiderwebs that laced the neatly mowed manor house lawn. It appeared that a new gardener had finally been hired, since everything looked spit-spot. I felt a pang that Stone the fourth had to take care of the tedious day-to-day issues his wife had previously handled, but he was in the middle of a divorce, and it looked like he intended to keep the house. This was great news for me, because my carriage house had been a real windfall and I didn't want to leave Greenwich just as I was getting my business established.

It was a relaxing drive up the back road to the preserve—at least until the driveway came into view. The news crews had multiplied like ants in a kitchen, and the reporters wore anxious looks, as if they were gearing up to pounce on any hint of a story. As I maneuvered my car behind a van to park, a cameraman strode my way. I thought about calling Evie, but I didn't want to ask her to rescue me with the golf cart again. The poor woman had suffered enough already, and I wouldn't blame her if she was contemplating her own permanent escape from the preserve.

I stepped out and slammed my door shut, but before I could fully turn around, a microphone was shoved toward my face.

A short woman in a pencil skirt blasted me with a question. "Are you an employee of the White Pine Wolf Preserve?"

"No comment," I said, pretty certain this was the correct protocol. Sergeant Hardy would be proud of me.

I walked a few steps, but the cameraman and reporter cut in front of me. The woman jutted out her sharp chin as she spoke, a serious look plastered on her face. "The police haven't ruled the latest death a wolf-killing yet. Do you have any idea why?"

That was news to me, but I tried to keep my face serene. "No comment," I repeated, then jogged over to the gate.

Of course, the moment I tried the latch, I realized it was locked. And I didn't have the key.

The reporters pressed in on me, each question more urgent than the last. I had two choices—climb over the gate, which would probably afford an excellent shot of my derrière for the nightly news—or wade into the tight, brambly underbrush to the side of the gate.

I chose the underbrush.

As blackberry vines tore at my sweatshirt, I wished I'd stopped and called Evie, regardless of how traumatized she was. When I felt overwhelmed, I tended to make less-than-ideal choices.

As the barn came into view, it hit me that I was probably retracing the exact path the lurker in the parking lot had taken. Pushing against a blackberry vine, I was surprised to see something bright blue caught in it. I carefully unhooked the rubber wristband from the thorns. It was one of those personalized unisex bands, and it bore the words: *Two Hearts, One Love—The O'Callaghans, 6-18-2016.*

Had the bulky man lost it when he ran away from us? If so, it was a rather sentimental wristband for a man to wear. It must have meant something to him.

I tucked the band into my pocket. Feeling much the worse for wear, I yanked a final thorn from my sweatshirt and lurched up the driveway. When the reporters caught sight of me, they shouted questions over the gate, but I ignored them.

Sergeant Hardy stood by his police car, talking with Dahlia. I didn't have to be a body language expert to observe that they couldn't stand each other. Dahlia's hands were on her hips and she leaned in, her tone blistering hot. Sergeant Hardy held his notebook between them like a shield.

"We've canceled tours for the month and given a statement to the reporters—what more do you want from us?" Dahlia demanded.

Evie blocked the open gift shop doorway, so I figured I might as well settle in to hear whatever news the sergeant had brought. As unobtrusively as possible, I leaned over to fiddle with the shoestring on my boot, edging a bit closer in the process.

The sergeant's voice was tense. "As much as I wish this had been a wolf-killing—and trust me, I'd like nothing more than to shut your slipshod operation down permanently—the coroner's saying it wasn't. In fact, he's taken samples from Rich and Shaun and sent them to the toxicology lab. When he didn't find any mortal wounds on either of them, he suspected they might have been poisoned. So that means the wolves didn't kill Rich, and it's entirely possible they didn't kill Shaun, either."

Talk about a bombshell. Dahlia went white, and Evie rushed out to wrap an arm around her.

"You're quite positive?" Evie asked.

The sergeant nodded. "Yes, and what *that* means is that this is now a homicide investigation. We'll need to interview everyone properly down at the station—starting with you, Ms. White. I need you to get in the car with me."

I almost detected a note of glee in his voice. I was betting he'd been waiting to rake her over the coals since that time one of her wolves escaped.

Evie spoke firmly, as if she'd overcome her surprise. "I'll handle things here. You go on with the sergeant, Dahlia. Don't fret about a thing. Marco's already here, and Belinda's just arrived."

Evie nodded at me, and Dahlia turned her teary gaze my way. She looked like she hadn't slept any better than I had.

"Good." Dahlia took a deep breath and straightened. "Good. Of course I'll go down to the station, Sergeant. I have nothing to hide." She swept toward the police car with all the flurry of a winter storm.

Remembering the band in my pocket, I rushed over to Sergeant Hardy. "I forgot to tell you that Veronica and I saw a burly guy hanging around the parking lot yesterday when the gate was closed. He could've been a reporter, but he looked suspicious and bolted into the woods the minute we saw him." I pulled the blue wristband from my pocket and handed it to him. "This must've gotten yanked off when he dodged into the blackberry brambles."

I sensed Evie inching closer to my side, so I glanced at her. She was blinking rapidly, and she placed a clammy hand on my arm, as if to steady herself.

"I'm ready to go now," Dahlia yelled impatiently from the open police car window.

Sergeant Hardy sighed, balling the band in his fist. "I'll look into it. Thanks for the heads-up. If you see the man again, call me immediately. Evie has my direct line."

Evie gave a weak nod. Once the sergeant drove off with our boss in tow, I turned to the visibly shaken administrative assistant.

"What's going on?"

* * * *

Evie shook her head. "I'm not ready to talk about this yet. I need to make a call first. But I promise I'll explain more over lunch."

"Of course," I said, wishing I hadn't distressed her even further.

As she grabbed her phone from the desk, I went into the kitchen and donned my green vest, figuring I might as well get to work. I peered into the off-white fridge. The meat supply was definitely lower, and I had no idea where the vitamins were that Rich always added to the wolves' food. Who was in charge of ordering the meat in the first place? I was betting that had been Rich's job, as well.

I sank into a chair, feeling numb. Beyond the troublesome technicalities of trying to feed the wolves properly, I had a larger issue burning a hole in my brain. If Njord and his pack didn't kill Rich and maybe didn't even kill Shaun, then *who did?* Sergeant Hardy had said one or both the deceased could have been poisoned.

Which meant that the murderer might be an employee at the preserve. Although the bulky man from the parking lot *could* have crept into the woods at two different times to kill both men, it seemed highly unlikely. The murderer had to have been familiar with the gate system, not to mention the wolves themselves, since Rich and Shaun were found *inside* the enclosure.

A chill ran up my arms. Was I working with a murderer?

The door swung open and Marco walked in, wearing slouchy jeans and a green vest. He threw open the fridge door and started grabbing meats.

"Are you going to feed the wolves right now?" I asked.

He grunted his affirmation.

"Do you need some help with that?" I offered.

He gave me a measuring glance. "You've done this before?"

"Yes, I helped Rich a few times," I said. "I did the water, but I helped move the meats, too."

"Great. Then sure, load 'er up."

We worked in silence until the buckets were full. Things moved more quickly, because Marco was solidly built, hefting far more weight than Rich had been able to. Once we were done, I was relieved to see Marco adding the vitamin supplements to the food.

He gave me another once-over with his dark eyes. "Are you okay to go into the enclosures with me? If you could handle the water again, I can do the meats."

I hesitated, but only for a moment. Although I could hear Katrina's voice screaming at me in my head, I nodded. "Sure. I know the drill."

"Great." Marco pushed the wheelbarrow off toward the woods, and I trailed behind.

It was a risky move, sure, but if there was a murderer running around like Sergeant Hardy had said, I might actually be safer *inside* the wolves' enclosure than out.

15

As we approached the first enclosure, Freya trotted right up to the gate to meet us. She ignored Marco as he walked over to distribute the food, and instead she followed me to the watering trough, as if following some well-established routine.

It was endearing, and I couldn't resist patting her head. I noted that one of her ears had a tiny notch, like something had once bitten a piece out of it. She rubbed around my legs, then flopped into a heap at my feet, waiting for a tummy rub.

As the water filled the trough, I glanced down at her smiling golden eyes and her chocolate-brown coat. Her tongue lolled out to one side, and she had a contagious kind of happiness that lifted my spirits. I rewarded her with a thorough petting.

Thor had finished gobbling his food, and he tactfully sat down at Marco's feet, not even begging for a pet. The pack leader seemed to know something was amiss, and I was hit with a fresh wave of grief that Thor's best human friend was dead.

"Let's move on," Marco said, wheeling the buckets toward the fence.

I nodded and shut off the water, giving Freya a final scratch under her chin. She was the loving kind of animal that seemed like she'd make a good pet, yet that kind of thinking had led to the ultimate abandonment of most of these wolves. People had thought they could tame the wolf out of them, but at some point they'd had to admit it was impossible.

Marco rolled along in silence. I attempted a little small talk, since I'd have to be working with him for several more days.

"So you've known Dahlia for a while?" I asked.

He shot me an unreadable look over his shoulder. "Yeah. She had big dreams, you know? And she's come so far—building up this place, redoing the barn, advertising—you name it."

I noted the pride in his voice. Obviously, he'd bought Dahlia's savior-of-wolves story. Were Rich and I the only ones who had noticed that she was never in the enclosures with her beloved animals?

"You were the one who located the wolves for her, right? How did you go about doing that?" I asked.

Marco plodded along, his back to me. "That's not important, and it's not something I share with Dahlia or with anyone. The point is, I always know she's going to get those wolves healthy and take good care of them."

I remembered Carson's accusation that Marco had ties to the black market of wolf fighting, and Marco's response did little to dispel that notion.

I tried another tack. "Why doesn't Dahlia let Carson help with the wolves?"

Marco slowed, violently bumping the wheelbarrow tire out of a muddy area and back onto the path. "She protects him like a little baby. I've told her to make him carry his own weight around here. But she says Carson has to pursue a more intellectual line of work since he's gotten his fancy geology degree. Seems to me that degree ain't worth the paper it was printed on."

I had to agree. Carson seemed unmotivated, stagnant in the life his mom had foisted on him.

"His grandpa agrees with me," Marco continued. "He wants Carson to come and work at his construction company. It would be office work—nothing really labor-intensive. But Dahlia will have none of it. She can't stand the thought of her son working for her ex's dad."

Based on my only run-in with Dennis Arden, I figured he wasn't champing at the bit to employ his grandson, either.

At the gate of Njord's enclosure, Marco whipped out a key and inserted it in the new lock. Njord and the sibling wolves saw us and rushed toward the second gate, forming a loose line in front of it.

I hoped my apprehension didn't show as I pushed the gate open for Marco to wheel through. While this pack might not have killed anyone, they'd undeniably chewed on Shaun and attacked Carson's hand. We were stepping right into an enclosed space with these animals.

Marco didn't waver as he rolled the wheelbarrow straight toward the food dish. I followed his example and walked directly to the spigot. Unfortunately, Njord ignored Marco and sidled alongside me, frisking about like he'd done for Rich. I tried not to focus on the sharp teeth in his open mouth. Instead, I murmured, "You're a good wolf, aren't you, boy?"

Njord gave a little yip and my stomach nearly dropped to my feet, but I kept my back to him and ran the water. Once the trough was full enough, I walked over to the gate, thankful to see Marco standing there waiting for me. He was holding something in his hand and I took a second look at it.

It was his canister of pepper spray.

I'd never even thought of pulling mine out—in fact, I'd all but forgotten each green vest was equipped with one.

Marco held up the canister and shrugged. "Can't be too careful. I know these wolves, that they're good animals, but they're still wolves. Doesn't hurt to have some protection at the ready."

I nodded my agreement, walking ahead of Marco so he could lock the gates behind us. As we exited the final gate, Carson rudely speed-walked past us without saying hello. He was heading deeper into the woods and was clearly in a hurry.

"Do you mind if I take a minute?" I asked Marco.

Marco's gaze traveled to Carson's retreating back. "Go ahead. Just don't let him near the enclosures. You saw what happened to him yesterday when he decided to pet the wolves."

"Right. Thanks. Are you heading home soon? If so, I can feed the smaller animals."

He nodded. "I had planned to check the meat supply, then I should get going, since I'm in Manhattan. Dahlia seemed confident you could handle the hobby farm animals alone?"

"Definitely. I really appreciate your making a trip in to help out. See you tomorrow."

As Marco rolled the wheelbarrow down the path, I walked to the top of the small hill. Cupping my hands together, I shouted, "Carson! Could I talk to you just a minute?"

Carson was nearly out of view, but he stopped and turned. "What?"

I shouted louder. "Could you come here a minute?"

He gave a reluctant nod before backtracking to meet me. "I'm kind of in a hurry," he said, cradling his bandaged hand as if it hurt terribly.

I wondered what was propelling his urgency. I hadn't seen Veronica today, but maybe she'd gone out on a morning jaunt and Carson was trying to catch up to her.

"How's the hand?" I asked.

He adjusted his glasses. "The doctors say it's a miracle those beasts didn't take off a finger." As he spoke, he didn't even look at the wolves in question.

Unlike Carson, I couldn't help stealing a glance at Njord and his gang. They were curiously watching Carson's every move.

I refocused on the conversation, which was actually a type of private interrogation. "Can you tell me what happened again? You were trying to explain things yesterday, but I was focused on getting you back to the visitors' center."

I'd just given him a prime opportunity to offer me some thanks, but he didn't. Instead, he launched into his traumatic tale with relish. "Yes, I was trying to pet the white wolf, Njord. He's always seemed so friendly with Rich. I had just petted Njord—through the fencing, mind you—when next thing I knew, the freaking wolf had my hand clamped in his jaws. I had to use my other hand to pull it out, but by that time the other wolves had gathered and they'd started nipping at me, too. You saw what they did to my hand."

I nodded. "I'm so sorry. The wolves were definitely behaving strangely with you. They're not normally like that."

Carson sniffed. "I hate my mom's uncontrollable wolves, but I can't talk her into getting rid of them."

Why had he tried so hard to pet wolves he didn't even like in the first place? He must be desperate to prove his competency on the preserve.

I shrugged. "Maybe you could move away—you know, get a job elsewhere."

He tucked his Oxford-cloth shirt into his jeans. "I haven't found one suited to me yet. I have a Yale degree, you know? I'm overqualified for most things."

I struggled to hide my surprise. Carson's degree was from Yale? Why wasn't he working some big-time job? "And what is your degree in?" I asked, acting like Marco hadn't already told me that Carson had a geology degree.

"Geology. I haven't decided if I want to go back and get my master's yet. Veronica keeps encouraging me to do it."

"Getting your master's would likely mean you'd have to leave home, so your mom would have to manage the preserve on her own," I said.

"Yeah…" He cast an anxious glance into the woods. "I have to go now. Oh, by the way, how'd you like Marco?"

"He seemed nice enough," I said.

Carson gave a twisted smile. "I see he's fooled you, too. He's a con man, if you ask me."

"You have any proof?" I asked.

Carson was already walking away, but he turned. "No, but maybe I can get some," he said enigmatically.

16

I was nearly back to the visitors' center when Veronica approached in the golf cart, driving far too fast. I jumped out of the way as she ground to a halt.

"I'm sorry, Belinda! I've only driven this once before, and as you can see, I don't have the hang of it yet."

She was so apologetic, I shook my head. "Don't worry about it." I glanced at the dashboard, which was extremely basic. "You want me to give you a few pointers?"

She shot me a grateful look and slid into the passenger's seat. "Would you? Have you driven this before?"

I climbed into the driver's seat. "No, but I drive four-wheelers and snowmobiles back at home. This thing's electric, and it looks a lot easier."

"Where's your home?" she asked.

I didn't know where this newfound spirit of rapport was coming from, but I was slowly warming to it. "I'm from upstate New York—a little town called Larches Corner."

"Cute," she said. "So, why do you drive four-wheelers and stuff—do you live on a farm?"

"Well, my parents sort of have a hobby farm, and I like to drive around on their property." I thought back over all the animals my mom had raised over the years, including the turkey we butchered this past Thanksgiving. "Hobby farm" didn't quite capture the scope of Mom's endeavors, but we also didn't have a working farm like Jonas.

"How quaint," Veronica said, and I bristled at her tone, which made it sound like I was some kind of hillbilly. "I grew up in the city, but I've learned so much from working at White Pine," she continued. "I really hope I don't get sacked. I've hit the jackpot with this job, as far as finding examples for my thesis."

I brushed my hurt feelings aside and turned off the cart so I didn't waste electricity. "Why would you think you'd get sacked? Dahlia seems to like you."

"She does, but Sergeant Hardy would rather I didn't stick around, since I'm basically unnecessary personnel."

"He told you that?" I asked.

Veronica grinned. "He did. I haven't shared this with anyone yet, but Jacob—Sergeant Hardy—and I are dating." She bumped my shoulder with her own. "To tell you the truth, we were actually dating *before* all these wolf attacks started up."

That explained so much about Veronica's come-hither glances and the sergeant's subdued responses to her open flirtation.

"You don't say," I said. "Does Carson know this?"

"Carson Schmarson," she said spitefully. "Carson is a *boy.* Jacob is a *man.*" She gave me a long look. "Do you want Carson? You can certainly have him."

I laughed. "Uh, no. Nothing could be further from the truth. Anyway, how did you and, uh…Jacob…meet?"

"At a restaurant where I work part-time. He was sincerely interested when I told him about my life, and he left me a huge tip…and his phone number. We've been seeing each other ever since."

"Doesn't that compromise his investigation now that it's a homicide, though?"

Veronica's eyes widened. "Homicide? This is a murder investigation? But why? The wolves killed Rich and Shaun, right?"

Apparently, Sergeant Hardy hadn't kept Veronica abreast of the facts, which made me wonder how tight the two of them really were.

"It was a new development as of this morning—he said they're checking into other methods of death. There was no evidence the wolves had harmed Rich, and even though they'd obviously chewed on Shaun, it's possible they didn't kill him."

Veronica slumped back in the golf cart seat, her ponytail swaying. "You don't say. I'm sure Jacob was disappointed."

I was confused. "But why? Surely he'd want to get to the truth?"

"Well, yeah, he definitely wants to catch the killer, but he would have liked to shut this place down, too. We were hanging out with his officer friends one night, and I overheard one of them mention that Jacob lost his only sister several years ago—to a dog attack. That's why he's so hypervigilant about what's been going on at the White Pine Wolf Preserve."

That would explain why Sergeant Hardy and Dahlia had clashed so publicly a couple of years ago, when one of her wolves was on the lam in the back yards of suburbia.

Veronica swept her damp bangs from her forehead. "It's getting hot. Now that I know the wolves probably didn't kill people, I can get a little closer for my research."

"You've gone in by yourself before?" I asked, suspicion racing through me. I hadn't considered that Veronica might be comfortable enough to let herself into the wolf enclosures…which meant she could fit the profile of the killer.

"I have. I wanted to check in on them today, and now that I know it's safe to go into the enclosures, I'll just grab the keys from the kitchen. Were you heading back that way?"

I nodded, trying to overcome my sudden uncertainty toward the grad student. "How about if I drive us around a couple of times so you can get a feel for this golf cart?"

"Sure, I'd appreciate that," she said.

As I turned the golf cart on and hit the gas, I mentally listed reasons why Veronica probably wasn't the killer. Unlike most people here, she had been very up-front with me, and she'd given me quite a bit of information to chew on. I couldn't imagine any possible motive for her to kill Shaun and Rich, and she didn't seem the type to take people's lives.

After driving around the loop through the woods, I let Veronica take over. She slammed the brakes a couple of times, but eventually she got the hang of it. I warned her that Carson was lurking in the woods somewhere, but she shrugged it off, saying he was too scared to follow her into Thor's enclosure anyway.

"I'm glad you're getting closer to the wolves," I said. "I remember Rich told me you were good with them."

She pulled up next to the visitors' center. "I actually find it relaxing to hang around them—well, at least I *did*, before these attacks started. The wolves are playful, and they aren't stingy with their love. I'm sure that's the way Rich felt about them, too. And Shaun was one of those live-for-the-moment kind of guys who just loved everyone and everything. I think he even had a little crush on you." She winked.

"Shaun was sweet, and he certainly didn't deserve that kind of death." I had a sudden brainstorm. "Listen, since you won't be taking tours out for a while, would you like to train to help with feedings? Marco does the majority of the heavy lifting and he handles the wolves' meats, but I could show you how to fill the watering troughs and maybe how to feed the smaller animals." It wouldn't hurt to have backup for when my term on the preserve ended. If Veronica could handle my chores, Dahlia would be less likely to ask me to extend my contract.

Veronica didn't hesitate. "Of course. I could explain to Jacob that you need my help, so I'd need to stick around—which is what I want, anyway. How about tomorrow?"

"You've got it," I said, hopping out of the cart by the front door.

Veronica waved and pulled around to the side door to grab the wolf enclosure keys.

As I walked into the gift shop, my spirits were buoyant. Evie strode over from behind her desk. "Are you ready to eat?" she asked.

My stomach rumbled. "Definitely."

* * * *

The taco restaurant promised to become one of my new favorite places to eat. As the waiter sprinkled salt on the freshly made chunky guacamole, Evie and I made small talk about the weather. But when he finally strode off, Evie shot me a serious look.

"I've looked into things, and I think I know who the man was in the parking lot," she said.

I munched on a nacho. "Who is he?"

"My ex," she said, sighing. "The last I'd heard, he was in prison. Yet the past couple of weeks, I couldn't shake the feeling that someone was watching me. I told myself I was just imagining things. I actually called the prison—that day you first came—but I had to leave a message, and no one got back to me, so I tried to brush off my misgivings."

She paused as the waiter refilled her iced tea, and when he left, she resumed her story. "When I heard what you said to Sergeant Hardy, I realized maybe my gut instinct was right—maybe someone has been stalking me. I made a call to the prison, and they had misplaced my message. It turns out my ex was released three weeks ago."

"He's tracked you down?" I asked.

"So it would appear. I don't know how he scrounged the funds to come here. I thought I'd be safe in the States."

"Wait—you mean you came all the way to the U.S. to get away from him?"

"Yes. I didn't adopt a pseudonym or anything like that, although I did go back to my maiden name. In retrospect, it seems I should have legally changed my name and done a better job hiding. I just assumed he wouldn't get out for years and that he'd never have the money to fly over and find me." She took a long drink and frowned. "My divorce lawyer wasn't the best—he should have been the one to let me know about the prison release."

"What did your ex-husband do to you?" I asked.

She shrugged. "He beat me. But that wasn't why he went to prison. He was embezzling from his firm, and once they discovered it, they made sure he was prosecuted to the fullest extent."

I finished my bite of steak taco. "And the blue wristband gave it away? I noticed how you flinched when you saw it."

She gave a brief nod. "It was from our wedding. He wore it, even when he was on trial. His way of saying that he owned me." She rubbed her thin upper arms. "And now it's clear he knows where I'm working."

"You have to tell Sergeant Hardy," I said. "Do you think your ex could have…well, could he have killed Shaun or Rich, maybe to get to you somehow?"

She nibbled at her adobo chicken enchilada. The lemon cream sauce had congealed a bit, but she didn't seem to care. "I don't think Brian would be capable of it, but then again, I'm an expert at underestimating him." Her matter-of-fact manner evaporated, and I saw desperation in her eyes. "How am I supposed to continue working at the preserve, now that he knows where I am?"

"I'm sure if you told Sergeant Hardy, he'd come up with some way to protect you," I offered.

Evie rubbed at her forehead, as if staving off a gargantuan headache—which was essentially what her ex was. "But what if Brian follows me home *tonight*? I don't have any kind of weapon. Even my kitchen knives are dull."

I had a crazy brainstorm. "You can come home with me," I said. "I have a couch that pulls into a bed."

She smiled, but shook her head. "What about the next night, and the next? I can't move in with you, Belinda, although I appreciate the sentiment. It would be best if I packed up and moved altogether."

"You'd need to land another job first," I said. My wheels were turning, and as usual, I improvised. "Listen, I have some friends and they have plenty of extra rooms in their home. They also have top-of-the-line security. Why don't I ask them if you could settle in there for a short time? If they agreed, I could drop you off at their place after work."

"And my things?" she asked.

I placed my hand on her arm. "I know someone, and if I haven't missed my guess, he could retrieve your things for you *and* deal with any kind of hassle Brian dishes out."

She gave me a pained gaze. "That is very kind of you. I'm so sorry to put you in this position. It seems I'm always leaning on others, especially after I finally got away from Brian."

"Sometimes leaning is the only way to stay upright," I said. "We'll get you taken care of."

17

I had never been more thankful I'd followed up on my urge to have lunch with Evie; otherwise, she might have never opened up about her abusive ex. I dropped her off at the visitors' center, then sat on a rocking chair outside and made couple of calls.

First, I asked Ava if she would mind if Evie stayed over. After hearing Evie's story, Ava agreed that she could stay indefinitely while she figured out her next steps. I had correctly guessed that my generous friend would open her home to someone in need.

I called Red next. He said he was grabbing lunch at The Apricot Macaron before heading into Manhattan to pick up Stone the fourth from work.

I laid my cards on the table. "Red, I know you were in the army. I also know you carry weapons—don't worry, they're not obvious. I just notice things like that. Anyway, I work with this woman who just found out her crazy British ex has tracked her all the way to America, and now he's stalking her. She's going to stay with some of my friends tonight—the Fentons, if you remember them—but I wondered if you would be able to pick up her things and get them over to her at some point? There's a chance you might run into her ex, though."

I figured that voicing my hesitancy might make Red step up to the plate, and he did. His voice roughened. "The ex will not be a problem. Just give me the address and a list of things she needs, and I'll get over there tonight."

"I'll get her key to you first," I said.

"Not necessary, but okay."

Once again, I wanted to ask Red just exactly what he had done in the army, but I held back. I wasn't quite sure I wanted to know.

After thanking him, I hung up and headed into the visitors' center. Evie was on the phone. She held up her finger, and I waited until she finished her conversation.

"Sergeant Hardy doesn't have anyone to spare, but he will have someone drive by the preserve daily. That was all he could promise," she said, looking defeated.

I was grateful I had good news to share. After telling Evie that the Fentons were happy to take her in, I mentioned that Red was also willing to gather whatever things she needed from her place and drop them by later.

"You're a miracle worker, Belinda! I'll never be able to thank you enough," Evie said, pulling me into a hug. She retrieved her key chain and pulled off a key, writing down her apartment address for Red.

Happy to have put Evie's mind temporarily at ease, I headed into the kitchen and grabbed my vest. But as I walked out, my steps grew heavier as I thought of each question that was still unanswered. Did Shaun have pepper spray in his vest when he died? Did Rich? Were the men poisoned, or had they died from some other cause? What had spurred the wolves to gnaw on Shaun and attack Carson?

I hoped Sergeant Hardy would fill us in soon.

* * * *

I'd only been in the chicken coop for two minutes when it became clear that some days, the chickens could be an even bigger handful than a pack of wolves. Two chickens were having a fierce stare down over an egg, one was determined to get out of the fence by relentlessly running straight at it, and an undersized white chicken followed me around, pecking at my legs.

It seemed to me the drawbacks of having chickens far outweighed the benefits, but maybe I just wasn't a chicken person.

By the time I'd fed the frisky goats and braved the endless peacock shrieks, I was ready to hit the Dunkin' D drive-through for a large iced coffee. It would be great when Veronica learned to do these chores, because she could take some of the load off me.

The wooden peacock fence adjoined Dahlia's manicured back lawn, and when the birds miraculously fell silent, voices drifted my way. Two people were deep in conversation in Dahlia's backyard. I listened closely, silently trying to shoo the rustling peacocks toward their food so I could hear better.

I recognized Dahlia's voice. "I'm afraid we'll have to move," she said. "Dennis will be thrilled to get his claws back on his property—he hated that Quinn included it in the divorce settlement."

The deep, soothing voice that responded was not at all who I'd expected: Marco Goretti. Apparently, he hadn't gone home as early as he'd planned.

"Quinn can't renege on what he gave you in the settlement," Marco said. "Besides, you know if you are forced to sell and move out, you can always move in with me. You like my brownstone, right?"

Dahlia sniffled. "But it's not big enough for all three of us."

Marco's voice took on a hard edge. "Carson's old enough to be on his own. You should be charging him rent as it is; maybe that would force him to get out and get a job."

Dahlia muttered incoherently.

I snuck closer to the fence, willing the peacocks to stay quiet.

"That geology degree hasn't really paid off yet," she said. "It just puts him at a disadvantage when he's job hunting, you know."

"He's lazy," Marco said firmly. "He never even did the work-study program at Yale like he promised. He let you foot the bill for everything."

"Well, but..." Dahlia sputtered. "It was all his father's fault. Quinn was never there for Carson, never went to any of his concerts or chess tournaments. That's why Carson finds it so hard to trust you, Marco. He saw how his father treated me. Quinn has more than enough money, but he expected me to pay for Yale. I'll be in debt for the rest of my life."

"We'll work through this together," Marco murmured. They both fell silent. It was possible he'd pulled her into a comforting hug.

I quietly exited the peacock gate, astounded by this unexpected alliance. I would never have guessed it, based on the story Carson had shared about Marco's illegal connections. Now I saw that Carson could have been exaggerating, even shifting blame due to issues with his own father.

What if the murderer's end goal was to make the White Pine Wolf Preserve fail? Marco wanted Dahlia to move in with him, but she had resisted since Carson was still home. Would that be a strong enough motivation to kill, so Dahlia would have to close up shop and find a new place to live?

It seemed unlikely, but I remembered that Katrina had once mentioned that killers rarely had logic that made sense, no matter how much sense it made to *them*.

My list of possible suspects was growing by the minute.

* * * *

After getting Evie settled at the Fentons', where she was welcomed with open arms, I headed out to Bluebell and gave Jonas a call to figure out when he was coming over. When he picked up, I heard the familiar bustle of New York City in the background.

"How's your Saturday?" I asked.

"It's been great. I've sold nearly all my stock," he said. "What time do you want me to head your way?"

"I'll be home in about five minutes, then I'll need to shower and cook, so how about six or thereabouts?"

"Six would work great. I'm going to need a shower, too, and it's a little drive to my bed-and-breakfast. I'll see you soon."

I hung up and ran through the drive-through for my coveted iced coffee, then made a beeline for my carriage house. After straightening the potted plants on my doorstep, I went inside and took a quick shower. To save time, I mentally rehearsed the preparation steps for my meal. Thankfully, I still had a large portion of Susan's lemon pound cake left for dessert, so that was one less thing I had to worry about.

After toweling off, I used a curl-defining lotion on my hair, then did my makeup. Finally, I donned my new green-embroidered peasant blouse and a ruffled skirt. I studied the finished product in my full-length mirror, adding dangly gold earrings for a sparkly touch. I looked a bit weary, yes, but my skin had picked up a tan from all the outdoor work, and the freckles sprinkling my cheeks gave me a healthy appearance. My naturally blonde hair had lightened a bit in the sunshine, too. In short, I looked like myself, which would probably be reassuring to Jonas, who was doubtless worried about the stressful effects of my wolf-tending job.

Tying an apron around my neck and waist, I launched into my meal prep. I'd decided on chicken cacciatore, which was simple and filling, yet classy. Sort of like Jonas himself—a dairy farmer with a penchant for classics and philosophy. I'd also prepped bacon-wrapped asparagus and new potatoes with garlic whipped butter, so it didn't take me long to throw things together.

I had just added the chicken to the tomato sauce when three knocks sounded on my door. I liked the sound of those knocks—self-assured and firm. Plus, he'd knocked three times so I was sure to hear.

I fluffed my curls and glanced around. Everything was in order. The table was set with my best plates and glasses, I had a bottle of sparkling cider chilling in the fridge, and cheese and fruit were arranged on my favorite rose-painted metal tray on the coffee table. My heart gave a little hitch as I walked to the door, anxious to see Jonas's face again.

As I swung the door open, he said, "Belinda."

There was something about the way his voice caressed my name. It seemed to insinuate that we were very close, that he knew me better than anyone.

As my eyes trailed down to the object he was standing next to—a vintage bicycle with a large red bow on it—it was indisputable that Jonas certainly did know me well.

He gave me a sheepish look, his silvery blue eyes twinkling. "I thought you might want this—you said you wanted to get more exercise, and I found this old bike of Mom's in the shed. She was happy for you to get some use out of it."

The vintage bike had obviously received a lot of tender loving care, and it sported a fresh coat of Tiffany blue paint. I ran my hand along the white seat, unable to resist the bike's pull. I steered it down the steps, bumped up the kickstand, and took it for a spin around my driveway.

Jonas, who wasn't one to smile frequently, wore an expectant grin as I pulled to a stop and dismounted. "You like it?"

"I love it! I especially like that I just have to backpedal to brake. I've always hated all those newfangled hand brakes."

He nodded. The dark hair on his shaved head had grown in a little, and his beard was neatly trimmed. Although he wasn't as tall as Stone the fifth, he had a compact type of barely bridled power about him. Whereas Stone was long-limbed with ropy, tennis-player muscles, Jonas had the kind of upper body build that evidenced his heavy-lifting farm life. He hefted my bike onto the porch with one capable hand and set the kickstand. A flash of desire surprised me—the urge to feel those strong hands around my waist.

I dunked my head, so my curls draped the sides of my face. I could only hope my flush was hidden. "You ready to eat?" I asked brusquely.

"Definitely." His eyes skimmed across my rosy cheeks—my discomfiture hadn't gone unnoticed, but he didn't mention it. "Let me just grab something from my truck first."

He ran out to his newer-model black truck and retrieved a small flowerpot with some kind of frilly green plant in it. Holding it out to me, he said, "I brought you some of our pink poppies. They're just starting to come up, but I think it's okay to plant them at this point. I noticed you were always telling Mom how you liked them."

I took the pot and caressed the pale, cabbage-like leaves. I couldn't actually think of words to express how much Jonas's gifts meant to me. They hadn't cost a fortune, but the thoughtfulness and effort behind them, as well as their reminder of his sweet, ailing mother, made me tear up.

I swiped at my eyes. "Jonas, I just…thank you so much. I'll plant these soon, probably in my back flower bed. They'll make me smile every time I look at them." Without thinking, I reached out to hug him.

My breath caught when he pulled me into a tight embrace, although it didn't slide into something sensual. Rather, it felt like we both craved some key element that only the other possessed.

I stayed that way, my head pressed tight against his heart and my arms wrapped around his sturdy back, until he released me. Neither of us apologized for our clinginess.

I led him inside, ready to get caught up with this man who seemed to instinctively know the things I valued most. Farmer Jonas Hawthorne was definitely one of a kind.

18

While Jonas wasn't thrilled with my wolf preserve updates, I could tell his interest was piqued as I elaborated on what Veronica had told me.

He swallowed a bite of asparagus, which he'd raved about. "So you're telling me that Sergeant Hardy is anti-wolf since his sister died of a dog attack? That's a strong motivation—if you're vengeful enough—to try to get the preserve shut down. Did he have any opportunity to kill Shaun or Rich?"

It was an outrageous idea—that a police officer would mastermind these killings—but it wasn't an impossibility, I supposed. Anyone could have snuck onto the preserve the morning Shaun died. Maybe Shaun had showed up way too early so he could meet with someone in private. Although Evie also tended to arrive early, she rarely left the visitors' center, so it was unlikely she would have noticed if someone was creeping around the paths to the wolf enclosures.

On the day Rich had died, Sergeant Hardy had gone to Njord's enclosure on his own, so there had been a brief window of opportunity when he could have attacked and killed Rich. He might have dragged Rich's body into the enclosure before hustling out the gates to pretend he was nearly as fresh to the scene as I was. It was also possible that in his hurry, he had left the gates unlocked, so he might have decided to shoot the opened locks off to cover his tracks.

I shared my half-baked theory with Jonas, and he furrowed his dark eyebrows. "It might be a long shot, but it does seem to explain a few things." He frowned. "If he's responsible for the deaths, then you aren't safe at all, Belinda. He could easily drop in to 'check on' something and do the same thing to you, if he wanted."

"But that's the question, isn't it? I mean, how many people would he need to kill to be sure he's ruined Dahlia's wolf preserve? She's already been hit with all kinds of bad press, so she's had to shut down tours. Honestly, I don't see how the preserve can recover." I chewed a bite of chicken, pleased with its tenderness, then washed it down with cider. "Come to think of it, Sergeant Hardy is the lead detective. Logically, if he killed Shaun and Rich, he's going to be busy trying to pin the murders on someone else."

Jonas looked thoughtful. "But if he was the murderer and he's controlling the investigation, why draw attention to the fact that Rich was murdered? Wouldn't he want to make sure it looked like the wolves did it?"

My mind whirred along, picking up possibilities and tossing them aside, until I came up with an explanation that worked. "Maybe he didn't get as much time as he thought he'd have for Rich. Let's say he dragged Rich into the enclosure, hoping the wolves would gnaw on him like they did on Shaun. He had instructed his other officer to check the first enclosure during this time, so that got him out of the way. He figured he'd have plenty of time, but then I came along and threw a wrench in his plans."

Jonas nodded. "It's possible. And because the wolves didn't have time to chew on Rich, the coroner discovered it wasn't a wolf attack, and he started looking into other methods of death. I wonder if they've determined if he was poisoned yet—you said toxicology was checking on things, right?"

"Right. Maybe there will be some more conclusive report tomorrow. I would hope that Sergeant Hardy would update Dahlia, but if he's the killer, he'd likely sit on that information as long as possible." I stood and walked into the kitchen. "Do you want decaf?"

Jonas grabbed the dirty dishes and utensils and joined me. "I'd love some."

I placed my favorite mug under the spout and dropped a decaf coffee pod in. As I retrieved the creamer from the fridge, I said, "One thing that's been niggling at me is that the killer would have to be comfortable enough with the wolves to go *into* their enclosure. So that would indicate it's most likely someone on the preserve."

"Good point," he said. He was scoping out the lemon pound cake, which I'd artfully placed on a crystal dish. "All the more reason to be extra cautious if you stay there."

"Help yourself," I said. "I met a new friend and she gave me that cake—it's delicious. Actually, I think she gave me the cake first and then I made a new friend, in that order."

Jonas smiled. "Don't mind if I do. I'll cut a piece for you, too."

Once he'd offered me the largest slice, I gathered my coffee and cake and led him to the couch. He politely stood while I positioned my food on the coffee table and settled into the couch, then he sat down—so distractingly close, our legs were nearly touching. He scanned my larger TV and my game systems. "Still gaming, I see?"

If anyone else had said that, I would think they were speaking condescendingly, like I was some frivolous entertainment junkie. But Jonas said it with a gravitas that implied that my gaming should be taken seriously.

"I am. I'm still doing articles and blog posts, that kind of thing. Trifling stuff, really."

He shook his head. "There's a guy in our book club and he was asking if you were *the* Belinda Blake. He said you needed to be on Switch."

"The Nintendo Switch? I have one."

"No, not that. It's some kind of gamer channel online. I don't know—"

"You mean *Twitch*. Yes, I'm working on getting set up for that."

Jonas's jeans-clad leg now rested against mine, just the tiniest bit, but enough to let me know he didn't mind leaving it there. I had to fight the urge to place my hand on his knee, which seemed the natural response.

He took another bite of cake, then turned to face me. I had forgotten how impenetrable his gaze could be…it always enthralled me and made me want to plumb its depths. But his words were far from enigmatic.

"I'm telling you, this cake is amazing." He licked the last crumbs from his lips and cocked his head. "Belinda, have you thought about building your gaming business, just like you did your pet-sitting business? It would be far less hassle than the pet-sitting jobs you've landed recently."

I propped my feet up on the coffee table, confident that Jonas would never chastise me for a lack of decorum. Besides, I needed to separate my leg from his so I could have a little more breathing room—something I desperately needed for the full-on sensory overload Jonas had stirred up.

"Yes, I've thought about that. But right now, I like the pet-sitting gig, too. I enjoy staying somewhat plugged into Manhattan, and I have several loyal clients there. Also, you know how I love being outdoors. Kind of weird for a gamer girl, I suppose."

His face softened. "I like that about you. You're perfectly comfortable inside or out—there's never a boring moment with you."

We fell into an amiable silence as we finished our dessert. Finally, Jonas placed his plate on the coffee table. I figured he was going to say good night and head back to his bed-and-breakfast. He'd had a long day, too.

Instead, he asked, "What's your take on Jordan Baker? Was she really on Gatsby's side?" The way he looked at me, you'd think everything in the universe hinged on my opinion of the book.

Jonas's question launched an impassioned discussion on side characters' roles in *The Great Gatsby* that continued well into the night. I wanted to go on talking, but Jonas pointed out that my eyes were hardly staying open. He said he needed to get back to the bed-and-breakfast before the owner called to see if he was returning at all.

He helped me to my feet, and the way he clung to my hand, I wondered if he was going to lean in for a good-night kiss. But Jonas wasn't the type of guy who would take advantage of my solitary living situation. He gave my hand a quick but thrilling squeeze and released it. "Thank you for tonight," he said.

"When do you have to leave tomorrow?" I wanted to eke out every last minute I could with him. "Maybe you could head out this way and we could meet somewhere for breakfast." An even better idea hit me, and I bounced up on my toes. "Or you could drop by the preserve! That way you could meet some of the people I've been talking about. I'd really value your opinion on things."

He took a moment to consider. "I think I could do it, as long as I got out of there kind of early. Mom's expecting me around noon."

I grinned. "Sounds great. I go in around seven-thirty in the morning. You want to meet me then? It should be fairly easy for you to find—just look up directions for the White Pine Wolf Preserve online."

"I'll do that." He met my gaze and held it. "I'll look forward to tomorrow."

After flipping on the porch light, I watched as he climbed into his truck and drove off. I probably should have told the security guard, Val, that I'd have a late-night visitor, but I was sure Jonas was perfectly capable of explaining why he was making a delayed exit.

It was only as I was crawling into bed that I realized I had been humming nonstop since I'd locked the front door.

For the first time, I was actually looking forward to going to work in the morning.

* * * *

I woke to the pleasant sounds of birds twittering just outside my open window and someone mowing the Carringtons' already-pristine lawn. I stretched in the sunlight, taking a deep breath of the ocean-salt air that wafted in on a light breeze. It was shaping into a beautiful day to show Jonas around the preserve.

Jonas had seemed intrigued to see the lay of the land where I worked, and I was looking forward to introducing him to all the key players at my strange job. An outside opinion might help me see them through different eyes and bring to light any possible threats.

As I pulled up the wolf preserve driveway, I was pleasantly surprised to see that it was free of reporters, and although the gate was closed, it wasn't locked. I pushed it open, drove through, then pulled it shut behind me. Jonas's black truck was already parked outside the visitors' center. He arrived everywhere a little early—he would definitely get along well with Red.

I got out and walked into the visitors' center. Evie rushed over to greet me. I was pleased to see she looked well-rested.

"Once again, I have to thank you for suggesting the Fentons," she said. "I had a wonderful evening talking with them. They're actually familiar with the village in Britain where I grew up."

"I know they travel frequently. I'm so glad you had a good night." I glanced around, anxious to find Jonas. "Have you seen a man with a shaved head hanging around, by any chance?"

"I certainly did. I rather fancied he was looking for you, but Veronica came in, all distraught about the chickens, so he went to help her. Said he was a farmer or something."

Definitely Jonas. I grabbed my green vest, then hurtled out the side door toward the chicken coop.

As I drew closer, it became clear that something was very amiss. Veronica was standing outside the chicken fence, her mouth agape. She silently pointed toward the chickens.

Inside the fence, Jonas held a large stick, which he wielded in an attempt to shoo off a raccoon that was bristling in the corner. There was a sizeable hole torn in the fence directly behind the predator, indicating how it had managed to get in.

Veronica grabbed my arm. In a breathless tone, she said, "Oh, Belinda, can you believe it? I came in and these chickens were squawking and there was this huge raccoon, prowling inside the fence! It was trying to eat them!"

That much was obvious, but I patted her hand. "Don't worry. Jonas has dealt with these kinds of things before." I didn't add that he usually carried a gun when he did so. "I'll go see if I can help him."

Jonas turned toward me and motioned to a chicken with an apparent death wish—it kept pecking its way toward the raccoon instead of away from it. I grabbed the wayward bird while Jonas extended his stick and firmly bopped the raccoon on the head. "They can be so stubborn, especially when there's food involved," he said.

Sure enough, the raccoon didn't budge.

Veronica screeched, and I turned. She was pointing to another chicken that was making its way up the roosting ladder, which was right next to the raccoon. "Don't let it kill it!" she shouted.

I didn't know which was worse—the oblivious chickens or Veronica's hysterics. "Shh!" I hissed, as the chicken under my arm launched into a fresh burst of squirming. "We'll deal with it!"

Jonas jabbed at the raccoon, and I nearly died when the animal charged his leg in return. Undaunted, Jonas swept the sturdy stick into the raccoon's side, almost like he was hitting a golf ball. The raccoon was thrown backward, landing by the hole in the fence. Jonas moved in menacingly, his stick outstretched. The raccoon hissed and snapped, but appeared to realize it had been beaten. It retreated backward through the hole, ending its brief reign of terror.

I gave a sigh of relief and dropped the unruly chicken, which promptly raced into the henhouse.

Veronica was nowhere in sight. She must have made a run for it when the raccoon emerged on her side of the fence.

"We'll need to repair that," Jonas said, his voice calm as ever, although his shoes and jeans were covered in dust. "Do you know where any chicken wire is?"

I assumed it was in the shed, so we temporarily blocked the hole with the chicken ladder board and I led him to the red building. While he retrieved the supplies, I ducked into the visitors' center and found Veronica huddled in the kitchen. I assured her that everything was under control, then Jonas and I went out to repair the fence.

He chuckled. "That Veronica's quite the city girl, isn't she?"

"Apparently. I don't know why she went ahead and started feeding the chickens without me. I told her I'd train her."

"Don't stress it. A raccoon in the henhouse is no laughing matter. If you ever see it again, call animal control."

I put my hand on my hip as he twisted the wire together. "In other words, do as I say, not as I do."

He gave me a wry look and continued his repairs. Once he was finished, we made our way back to the visitors' center. Evie and Marco didn't seem to be around, and Veronica had vanished as well, so I decided to give Jonas a quick tour in the woods before he had to head home. I grabbed the key to the first enclosure, ignoring the new key clearly marked *Njord's Pack* in Evie's careful handwriting.

As we walked up the dirt path, I gave Jonas's side a playful jab. "Veronica was quite a convincing damsel in distress. I think she was checking you out."

He replied swiftly, his eyes fixed on the trees ahead. "Was she? I didn't notice. She's really not my type."

I had a burning desire to ask what on earth his *type* was, but I didn't give in to it. Instead, I started overexplaining, which I tended to do when my emotions swam to the surface. "So, I think we'll go into the first wolf enclosure—I'm sure those wolves are harmless enough. There's this female wolf named Freya and she seems to like me. Then we can drop by the second enclosure, but we won't go in."

"Still worried they're killers?" Jonas asked.

I slowed. "Come to think of it, I'm not sure. I know Rich wasn't killed by Njord's pack, and Shaun might not have been, but the fact remains that the wolves must have chewed on Shaun, just like they chewed Carson's hand."

"And they didn't lay a tooth on Rich. But you said he was like the alpha of Njord's pack, right? The one who'd raised Njord from a pup? It makes sense he wouldn't dare hurt his alpha—in fact, didn't you say Njord was standing sentry over him?"

"He was, but he was that way with Shaun, too." I picked up the pace, leading us to the first gate, which I unlocked quickly. Although I wasn't overly excited to go into Thor's enclosure, I did think his pack was trustworthy enough and wouldn't try anything, especially with two of us. Besides, Jonas could read animal behavior better than most, and he would easily pick up any wolfish vibes I didn't.

I decided to go ahead and water the wolves, since that was the routine they expected from me. As Jonas followed me to the spigot, Thor was the first to come to my side. He seemed restless, but not aggressively so. He trotted between us, angling for a head rub, I suspected.

Jonas gave him a light pet while I poured the water, but Thor meandered off into the woods. It had grown quite warm out, and he probably needed some shade.

Freya loped our way, a frisky bounce in her step. She ignored Jonas and made a beeline for me, rolling around on the ground by my feet.

"I'd say she likes you," Jonas said.

I gave in and stroked her stomach, telling Jonas the sad story of how she came to the preserve.

"Seems like Dahlia's doing some important work here." Jonas shut the water off for me, then scanned the enclosure. "She's done a good job with the fencing, too."

I gave a short laugh. "I guess she had to, after one of her wolves escaped."

Jonas was still serious. "That's right, you'd mentioned that. But there's a learning curve to everything, and what one farm—or preserve—does one way, another will do a different way. Totally depends on the animals, and sometimes you don't know until you try."

Jonas's observations made sense, and I felt somewhat guilty for bad-mouthing Dahlia's efforts.

"Things seem pretty clean, too," he added. "The animals aren't overcrowded, like they were at the preserve I visited out West."

"I hadn't realized you'd been to a wolf preserve before." Actually, I wasn't even aware that he'd been out West. Maybe he had traveled there during one of the years I was in the Peace Corps. Although we'd grown up near each other and our relationship felt quite transparent, it seemed there were still some things I didn't know about Jonas.

I gave Freya a final pat and motioned toward the gate. "Let me show you Njord's enclosure, then I know you need to get on home, since your mom's expecting you by noon."

He glanced at the time on his phone. "Sounds good. I don't stop a lot, so I should be able to make it in around three hours."

As I locked the first gate, I broached the topic I knew he'd been avoiding. "What's going on with your mom, Jonas? Are they going to try more treatments?" I avoided meeting his eyes, giving him space as he answered.

"Not right now. Her body's too weak and it's spread to so many lymph nodes, they're saying the double mastectomy must not have gotten everything." He leaned against the second gate. "They're also saying the cancer is inoperable at this point."

I finally dragged my gaze to his face, and his defeated, helpless look almost made me plummet into tears. I took a deep breath as I led the way out the last gate. Slowly turning the lock behind me, I wished I could lock up all the pain of Naomi Hawthorne's cancer just as effortlessly.

I managed to keep my voice steady. "Thank you for telling me. I hadn't planned to visit at Easter, but I think I'll come up. Do you think your mom would mind if I dropped in one day?"

Jonas gave me a stoic smile that further wrecked my emotions. "She'd love that."

19

Marco rolled up with the wheelbarrow loaded with meat as we were returning to the path. His gaze traveled from Jonas to me, but he didn't comment.

"I just watered Thor's pack and I can meet you at Njord's to water them, if you want," I offered.

"Sure. I'd appreciate it. See you in a minute." He walked toward Thor's gate, whistling a tune.

When we were out of earshot, Jonas said, "He seemed nice enough."

"I think he is," I said. "He seems genuinely concerned about Dahlia, if not for her shiftless son."

"Speaking of Carson—that's his name, right?—I haven't seen him anywhere. I can't believe he doesn't pitch in more around here. This operation certainly can't run itself."

"That's for sure." As we approached Njord's gate, the white wolf gave us a golden stare, sniffing at the air.

"He's intense," Jonas remarked, which was funny, because I hadn't even seen him looking in the wolf's direction.

"Yes, but I'm not even kidding you when I say Njord enjoyed playing around with Rich—even giving him kisses!"

"Oh, I believe you. Which backs up my theory that there's no way Njord would harm him. Whoever killed Rich didn't understand pack dynamics very well."

Jonas had vocalized the very thing that had been bothering me. Although the killer had been comfortable enough to go into the wolf enclosures, he hadn't been aware of how the pack actually *worked*.

Marco wheeled over to us. He must have fed Thor's pack more quickly than usual. "I got to thinking that I didn't know who your friend was," he said awkwardly.

Realizing that Marco might be concerned about my safety—or the safety of the preserve—I made the introductions. "Marco, this is Jonas Hawthorne, a friend from upstate New York. Jonas, this is Marco Goretti."

Marco nodded to Jonas, but his look was somewhat challenging. "Were you planning to go in?"

True to his unflinching nature, Jonas said, "I hadn't planned on it, but I'd love to."

I placed my hand on his arm. "Jonas, you don't have to—"

"If you're safe in there, I'm sure I will be," he said, striding in behind Marco.

I followed the men, wondering how Njord would react to Jonas. I didn't have to wonder long. When Marco rolled the wheelbarrow over to the feeding area, Njord ignored the food and padded toward Jonas instead.

Not a word was spoken, and I don't even think one look was exchanged between man and wolf, but what happened next astounded me.

As Njord drew close, he dropped his head and tucked his tail. He slowly lowered into a crouching position under Jonas's hand, as if waiting for one crumb of recognition. When Jonas bestowed a single pat on his head, the white wolf dropped and rolled over, exposing his stomach.

The wolf might as well have shouted, "You're my new alpha! I will follow you!"

Jonas's lips slid into a half smile, and he bent down to rub Njord's stomach.

I turned on the spigot, then walked over to join them. Njord's tongue was hanging out, and his eyes were closed.

"You've got to be kidding me. You just walk into the enclosure, with a wolf pack that doesn't know you from Adam, and suddenly you're like the pack leader?"

Jonas shrugged, as if this kind of thing happened all the time. And maybe it did on his farm—after all, one time I'd watched him walk up and shout right in a bull's face.

He stood, leaving Njord lying in his happy stupor. "I don't know. It's just this thing that sometimes happens. I tend to have this effect on children, most animals, and things that are a little skittish. I can't really explain it."

Now that he said it, I realized I'd personally experienced the power of Jonas's reassuring leader vibe, at least a few times.

"I guess that comes in handy," I said, still feeling awestruck. My dad was a vet and he was certainly confident around animals, but Jonas took things to a new level.

"My dad was the same way," Jonas said. "Although my brother, Levi, was kind of an exception. He chafed under Dad's authority."

"Levi started traveling right out of high school, didn't he? And now he's wound up in Alaska," I said. "Was that why? He was trying to avoid your dad?"

"Probably, but also the responsibilities of the dairy farm. Dad didn't expect Levi to take over, but I guess Levi always felt guilty that he didn't *want* to."

"Complicated," I mumbled.

"All families are," Jonas affirmed.

Marco's buckets were empty as he wheeled over to us. Njord stood, shook the dirt out of his fur, then trotted over to join Saga and Siggie at the food bowl.

Marco shot Jonas one of those respectful man-to-man looks. "I see you got along fine with the big boy," he said. Turning to me, he added, "Oh, and speaking of dangerous animals, I heard Veronica had a little trouble in the henhouse this morning." He broke into a laugh, slapping his leg.

Jonas nodded, but he was all business. "I repaired the hole in the fence, but you might want to make sure it's reinforced. That raccoon might try to get in the same way again."

Marco turned serious. "Will do." He gave Jonas's hand a quick, macho shake. "I appreciate your doing that. We're spread pretty thin around here. I don't know how much longer I'll be able to fill in—I'm supposed to be traveling next week."

I didn't ask Marco why he would be traveling—it was anyone's guess if his business was even legit in the first place.

"I'll be leaving next week, too," I said, hoping Marco would remind Dahlia I wouldn't be here indefinitely.

Marco shook his head. "Dahlia will have to start interviewing people, but who would want to work on a wolf preserve where two people have recently died?"

He had a valid point.

I tried to inject a little hope into the situation. "Maybe the police will have things figured out by then." If one particular police sergeant wasn't involved, that was.

"Maybe," Marco said, his depressed look revealing that he didn't think things would be squared away anytime soon. He rolled toward the gate.

I jogged over and turned off the spigot. Jonas fell in step beside me as I followed Marco out. After locking the gates behind us, Marco said he'd be glad to feed the chickens if I wanted to show Veronica how to feed the smaller animals today, so I agreed.

Marco tipped his head toward Jonas, then headed back toward the visitors' center. I glanced over at Jonas, feeling completely bummed that he had to go.

He seemed to be thinking along the same lines. "I hate to leave you here alone," he said. "Marco seems like a decent guy, and Veronica and Evie are probably harmless enough, but the fact remains that someone hanging around this preserve could be a killer."

"It still doesn't make sense why anyone would have killed Shaun or Rich. I mean, Shaun was just not the kind of guy who would tick anyone off. I wonder if the coroner was wrong and the wolves did kill him for some reason?"

Jonas sat down on an oversized rock, and I sank down next to him. "I doubt it, given the way you said he looked when you found him. It sounds like his body was largely intact—sorry for being gross—but they hadn't ripped into it as if they were actually going to *eat* him for a meal." He slapped the stone. "Hang on—what if someone poisoned him first, then before dragging him into the enclosure, they placed meat on him?"

That made more than a little sense. "That would definitely explain why the wolves chewed him up, but didn't eat more." There was a kink in his theory, though. "But what about Carson? The wolves gnawed on his hand when he was just trying to pet them. So maybe they only chew on people they don't respect as much? In that case, I still need to keep my distance. I'm not as high as you or Rich on their respect-o-meter."

Jonas looked frustrated. "You need to get out of here as soon as you can. It doesn't matter whether it's wolves or people killing people—the issue is that you're not safe on the preserve. Promise me you'll consider quitting." He glanced at his phone. "I really do need to head out. I'm so glad I got to see this place, though. It's not every day a random wolf gets friendly with me."

I met his eyes and he held my gaze. His serious, warm look seemed to loosen some of the knots in my spirit, and when he stretched out his arms for a hug, I gladly leaned into them.

He pressed a strong hand to the back of my head, holding my head against his chest. Then he briefly and unexpectedly dropped a kiss on the top of my curls. His voice was rough as he said, "Please take care of yourself, Belinda. Will I see you at Easter?"

I took one last, long whiff of his shirt, which smelled like clean laundry with a hint of something peppery, then extricated myself from his arms. "Count on it," I said.

Although I felt like falling back into Jonas and exploring the emotions I was pretty sure we both felt, these woods felt tainted. For all we knew, Creeper Carson might be watching us from the trees. This wasn't the right moment for us.

But something told me there was a right moment out there, and when it finally came to pass, I'd be every bit as eager as Njord had been to capture Jonas's undivided attention.

* * * *

By the time I met up with Veronica in the kitchen, she had calmed down and was recounting the raccoon story to Dennis Arden, who had apparently dropped by for the day.

I wished Dahlia would rope him in for some chores—although he was older, he looked hale and hearty—but I knew she'd never stoop to that, given her feelings for her father-in-law. And besides, he'd never agree to help her.

Why did he come around here anyway? Maybe to see Carson? Or to goad Dahlia? I remembered what Susan had mentioned about seeing a gray-haired man meeting with Dahlia in her bakery.

As Veronica bit into an interesting-looking veggie-laden taco, I opened my sandwich bag and turned to Dennis. "How's Carson today? I haven't seen him."

Dennis helped himself to a cup of coffee. "I haven't, either. Dahlia said he was out; I have no idea where. I'd hoped to talk to him. My construction company just picked up a big job over in New Rochelle, and I'm going to need someone to fill in at the office."

"That would be stellar." Evie seemed to appear out of thin air, but I suspected she'd been lurking and listening in the gift shop.

Dennis laughed. "You're trying to get rid of him too, are you?"

Again, I was shocked at how carelessly he spoke of his grandson, even though Carson was admittedly a slacker.

Evie adjusted her vivid emerald-green scarf. "I simply know how anxious Dahlia is for Carson to find work he enjoys." She turned and stalked back to the gift shop.

Dennis raised his eyebrows. "She's quite a pill, isn't she? Dahlia really knows how to pick 'em."

I wanted to stick up for Evie, maybe mention that Dahlia had chosen Dennis's own son as a husband, so how was that for poor picking? However, I managed to keep a lid on my snide remark and tried to redirect the conversation instead. "Does your wife help out with your business as well?" I asked.

His face fell. "Madeline died four years ago. But you're right—she did help at the company when she was well. She was the best secretary we ever had."

"I'm so sorry," I said.

His eyes crinkled behind his glasses lenses. "It's okay. You know, Madeline had big dreams for this property—she'd hoped to build a day spa here, complete with pools and English gardens…you name it. But then Quinn got married, and I gave it to him as a wedding present." He made a fist and pounded the table. "I can't tell you how many times I've regretted that decision."

Veronica stood and shoved her empty container in her lunch bag. For someone so tiny, she must have a hollow leg, given how fast she'd devoured three tacos. "I'm going to head out to the goat pen," she said.

I hurried to pack up my half-eaten lunch. "Um—you want to just stay outside the pen until I get there? I'll meet you in a minute."

Veronica shrugged. "Okay." She left through the kitchen door.

I turned back to Dennis and decided to go out on a limb. "Say, you haven't been over to that bakery in Stamford—The Apricot something or another—have you? Seems like I've seen you somewhere else."

I couldn't make out the expression in his eyes, but he didn't seem overly annoyed with my question. "Sure. It's a fantastic bakery. Croissants to die for. My Madeline would have approved—she had French blood in her."

I probed further. "I was thinking I might have seen you there with Dahlia?"

He shook his head vigorously. "No way on earth would I ask that woman into any restaurant with me. If she walked in, I'd walk right out—as soon as I could."

That level of distaste was hard to fake, so I had to assume he was telling the truth. I cleared my trash and stood. "Of course. I understand. Maybe I'll see you around there sometime."

He gave me a sharp, knowing look. "Does that mean you're not planning to be here long?"

I didn't see how that was any of his business. "I'm not sure."

He laughed and smacked his knee. "That greedy witch runs everyone out, sooner or later. Don't feel bad, sweetie."

Cringing at his overly familiar "sweetie," I gave a brief wave and headed out the kitchen door.

The more I hung around Dennis Arden, the more it seemed he was the one running his family off, not Dahlia. He seemed to have disdain for everyone, save his deceased wife, and it was decidedly possible he had painted their relationship in a way that reflected well on himself.

As I walked along the rock path to the goat pen, I tried to sort through what I'd learned so far. First, it could have been Rich who'd met and argued with Dahlia at The Apricot Macaron. But why?

I revisited the idea that Dahlia might be using her wolf preserve for nefarious purposes, given that Rich had said she wasn't really invested in the wolves' well-being. Dahlia's relationship with Marco, who had ties with unsavory characters, might back up that idea, but when I'd eavesdropped on those two, they hadn't mentioned anything illegal.

Then there was Sergeant Hardy, who had been the one to discover Rich's body. His sister had died of a dog attack, so he might have snapped if he suspected Dahlia's wolves were a danger to tourists…and more specifically, to his girlfriend, Veronica.

I still couldn't rule out Veronica, difficult as it was for me to consider her a serious suspect. As I approached the goat pen, I slowed to watch her interaction with the animals. Although she stayed outside the fence, she reached over to pet a friendly kid on the neck. She gave me a hearty wave when she caught sight of me.

"Hi! Isn't this little one cute? What do you call the goat babies?"

"Kids," I said.

"Aw. They're so adorable with their little tiny bleats. And those eyes— freaky!"

One of the goats nibbled at Veronica's jeans. "Don't let them grab your keys," I instructed. "I'm sure you already know this, but they'll eat anything."

Veronica obligingly stepped back from the fence. "How much feed do I give them?"

For the next little while, I showed her how to feed and water the goats. Veronica paid close attention to what I said, and when she fed the animals, I could tell her confidence was growing.

"How's your thesis coming along?" I asked.

She smiled. "Really well. I don't have much more to write. I just need another example or two."

I was jolted back into reality as I stared at her exultant face. It was all too easy to insert "another *death* or two" for "another example or two."

Surely no one in their right mind would consider killing just to score high on their thesis.

But who was I to determine if Veronica was in her right mind?

20

By the time I left for the day, Bluebell's leather seats had soaked up so much sunshine, they felt like they were melting my arms. Cranking the air conditioner, I whisked away from the preserve, wishing I didn't have to return.

Contractually, I only had four days left to work for Dahlia. And no one was holding me to it—if I determined I was walking out tomorrow, I could. But there was some kind of deeper loyalty to Shaun and Rich that was driving me to stay.

After all, if Sergeant Hardy was the killer, who was going to suspect him? I was pretty sure Dahlia didn't. Evie had been quick to obey his every command, probably hoping he'd boost his efforts to protect her from her ex.

And if Veronica was the killer, Sergeant Hardy likely wouldn't even investigate her, since he was dating her.

Maybe I could get closer to Dahlia tomorrow and try to probe a bit more into her motivations. It seemed most likely it was Rich who had publicly clashed with her at The Apricot Macaron, in which case, something Dahlia had said or done must have made him very upset.

I dropped by Whole Foods for a California roll, since sushi seemed light enough fare for tonight. As I pulled up at the Carrington estate, Val, the head of security, waved me over from his perch in the glassed-in booth. He leaned out as I rolled down my window.

"What's up?" I asked.

"Nothing. Just wanted to give you a heads-up that you have a friend here to see you—Dietrich Myers."

Dietrich was one of Stone the fifth's friends, but he had grown on me, as well. An acclaimed artist, he lived in the trendy section of Brooklyn called Williamsburg. He often dropped in for Stone's billiards parties, but since Stone wasn't around, my curiosity was piqued.

Dietrich was riding around on my bike as I pulled into my drive. He began to teeter as he braked, and I didn't want to think what would happen if the bike toppled over. Dietrich was dangerously thin, giving the impression that the smallest injury might do him in.

"Belinda, angel! This bike is so *extra*, with its darling paint job, wouldn't you say? Where'd you find this gem?"

"Someone gave it to me," I said, taking my sushi roll and shutting my car door. "Did you enjoy your ride?"

"Immensely," he said, parking the bike and walking over to me. He clasped his thin fingers around my arm, his gaze intense. As usual, his clothes emanated cigarette smoke. "Now, I know what you're thinking— *why* has Dietrich showed up at your whimsical Greenwich cottage out of the blue?"

I smiled. "You read my mind. But I'm happy to see you again. When was the last time you were here? December?"

"Yes, at our final billiards party, before Stone absconded to Bhutan."

"Easy for you to talk about absconding—you were the one who suggested the trip to him!"

Dietrich sighed. "I did, although I hated to see him go. But darling, I'll tell you that the yoga retreat set me on the path of the artist, so it was worth the exorbitant fee I paid for it."

I didn't want to argue with Dietrich, but I'd seen his outlandish artwork, and I thought perhaps the yoga retreat could have led him on a more edifying career path. His paintings featured misshapen people rendered in colors that brought to mind violent stomach viruses. I could hardly stand to look at them.

Yet strangely enough, he'd carved out a following that was eager to pay the high prices he set for his work. As my grandma would say, "Sometimes there's no accounting for taste."

"I'm glad you got to go there," I said.

He clapped and gave a little hop, as he often did when he was excited. "Now, I'll tell you why I'm here. Stone called and asked if I could find one of his documents and snap a picture of it for him. His dad's been working long hours in the city, so he thought I could drop in for that little errand and give the house a quick once-over, just to make sure everything's clean. They haven't hired a new housekeeper yet, so one of the local teens has been filling in. Stone wants to see if she's pulling her weight."

I unlocked my door, shaking my head. "That house is probably a bear to keep up with—I mean, given the sheer number of rooms, not to mention that sprawling, plant-filled conservatory. But why are you so happy about being sent on an errand just to check on his house?" I set my sushi roll on the kitchen counter.

"I'm dropping by my parents' house while I'm in Greenwich, so I'm multitasking." He withdrew a slim cigarette from the pocket of his slim-fit jeans, lit it, and took a deep puff. "But don't you see? He's coming back to us soon, I'm simply convinced of it."

I wasn't sure how Dietrich had connected taking a picture of a document and checking up on housekeeping with Stone's imminent return, but I nodded. "Okay, well, that's good."

Dietrich blew a smoke ring into the air, then let his inquisitive gaze rest on me. "I assumed you'd be overjoyed—weren't you and Stone an item?"

That was the problem. I never really knew with Stone. Had we kissed? Sure. But had it meant anything to him? I was completely uncertain.

Trying to divert Dietrich's attention, I opened the sushi container. "Would you like half a California roll?"

He shook his head. "Mother has an elaborate meal planned for me, and she's also invited a lineup of eligible and pedigreed Greenwich bachelorettes for me to peruse. She's determined to get me married off before I hit thirty." Taking my hand, he gave me an intense look. "Don't give up on him yet, Belinda. I know he'll return more focused than ever."

I nodded, dropping my eyes to hide my doubts. Sure, Stone would come back more focused…but what if he had no intention to focus on *me*?

* * * *

That night, Mom called to get an update on Jonas's visit, and I filled her in, letting her know I planned to come up for Easter.

"That's wonderful," she said. "You and Tyler can help me set up my new wind turbine. Your father thinks I can't do it."

As she explained all the benefits of her turbine, all I could think of was how dark the house was going to be on the days it wasn't windy enough to generate much power. Although Mom assured me her latest off-grid effort would provide ample electricity, I was pretty sure my dad would put his foot down when she actually got to the point of calling the electric company to cancel service.

Once, when I'd asked Dad how he felt about Mom's constant schemes to get back to nature, he'd said that although he would never stand in her way, he might reroute her path once in a while so that she wound up at the right place.

Katrina called not long after I hung up with Mom. I hadn't told her the latest, and when she heard that Rich and maybe even Shaun weren't killed by wolves, she immediately dug into the psychological aspect of things.

"Two murders? This isn't random, sis. Either someone had a motive for killing those specific employees, or someone could be a psychopath. We can't rule that out. Someone might have gotten a taste of killing with Shaun, then realized they liked it. They were more obvious the second time—leaving him in the wolf enclosure, but maybe more for show than to point at the wolves—sort of like a staged crime scene. The murderer is actually controlling the evidence he leaves behind. And Belinda, if it *is* a psychopath, then the murders will probably escalate."

She shouted at Tyler, who must have been in the other room. "Hon, would you mind bringing me some of those chocolate-covered almonds? They're in the cabinet!"

Returning to the conversation, Katrina said, "I can't get enough of those things. Now, pay attention—just watching your back might not be enough. The murderer might be clever, even charming. You can't trust anyone."

"You're always telling me that."

"It's because you don't listen! You just go charging into things." She crunched at her almonds. "Oh well. I can't warn you any more than I already have. How was Jonas? Mom told me about Mrs. Hawthorne—it's so sad. She used to give me fresh strawberries."

We swapped memories of Naomi Hawthorne until I realized we were acting as if the kindly woman were already dead. I was about to point that out when Katrina suddenly got irritated with the way Tyler was sorting laundry, so she said a curt good night and hung up.

I looked up psychopaths online, and what I read was chilling. They actually enjoyed violence—it made them feel calmer—and they were skilled liars. Just about anyone on the preserve might fit that bill, and I wouldn't even know.

Although Sergeant Hardy and Dennis Arden weren't always around, they both had strong motivations for seeing the White Pine Wolf Preserve permanently shut down. Veronica had a motive to gather case stories to back up her thesis. Evie and Carson...I wasn't sure. Maybe Marco had some underworld deals he couldn't afford to expose. I couldn't imagine why Dahlia herself would torpedo her own business, but if she was a psychopath, maybe there didn't have to be a reason.

Was this whole thing some kind of elaborate mind game? Had someone used the wolves to mask Shaun's murder, then decided they wanted the credit themselves?

If that were the case, it made sense that, like Katrina predicted, they'd kill again—this time making it obvious that it was their doing, and not the wolves'.

21

I woke to an early and persistent knocking at my door. Stumbling from my bed, I glanced down to make sure my pajamas were decent. I was wearing a retro *Castlevania* T-shirt and striped pajama pants I'd owned since high school—not the height of fashion, but not as risqué as some of my more holey T-shirts.

Trying to finger-pick my curls, I peeked out the front window. Red stood outside in his chauffeur hat and jacket, and he was holding some kind of box.

I opened the door and attempted a hearty welcome, but I hadn't had coffee, so my greeting sounded flat. Red didn't seem to notice as he extended the box toward me.

"For you, from Susan," he said. "I visited her place this morning, and she insisted I bring you a couple of her Scottish-recipe scones. She saw on the news that there's been a second death on that wolf preserve?" His jaw hardened, and he shifted into an almost protective stance.

I wished I could have Red tag along with me to work, bringing along whatever weapons and skills he possessed. However, I couldn't afford to employ him. He'd be like kryptonite to an overconfident psychopath, anyway.

And I wanted that murdering psycho to make some kind of disastrous mistake that would take him out of circulation and land him in prison.

With only a handful of us working at the preserve, the killer was likely to try again. I couldn't see any reason why he'd try to eliminate me, but I'd make sure the pepper spray was safely situated in my green vest before I went out to feed the wolves. No one had been murdered with a gun or knife yet, so hopefully the pepper spray would surprise the killer and allow me to get away.

But if he happened to be an employee, he would anticipate that I'd go for my pepper spray first. Maybe that's what had happened to Shaun and Rich. Had the killer somehow slipped the pepper sprays from their pockets before murdering them? Or had he poisoned them first, so they were incapacitated? I wondered if Sergeant Hardy would tell me if either of the men had a spray in their possession when they died.

Snapping back to Red's question, I responded, "Yes, there was another death. The police are all over it, though. No need to worry."

"Will the job be over soon?" He couldn't disguise the concern in his voice.

"Definitely. Just a few days now. Oh, and Red—did you get Evie's things over to her? I forgot to ask her yesterday, but I assumed you had."

He nodded. "It was no problem. I cleared the area before I went in and didn't find anyone lurking outside, but there were plenty of vantage points where a would-be stalker could hide out and keep tabs on her. You were right to get her out of there."

A shiver crept up my arms as I pictured Evie trying to fight off the larger-sized man I'd seen in the parking lot. It was a fight she couldn't win.

"I appreciate your help so much," I said.

Red gave me a no-nonsense look. "Call me if there's any trouble. I'm never too far."

"Thank you," I said, knowing he meant every word. "And please tell Susan thanks for the scones."

He nodded and walked over to his car. After waving good-bye and closing my door, I headed into the kitchen and cracked open the scone box, which was charming in and of itself. The same delicate shade as a fuzzy peach, the box had an overstuffed gold macaron stenciled on the lid. Unable to resist the buttery scent of the scones, I took the largest one out and bit into it. The texture was perfect, but the plain scone seemed to beg for more flavor. I went directly into the kitchen, retrieved some of Jonas's honey, and slathered it on.

Sitting down at my table to enjoy the honeyed scone and coffee, I rehearsed my plans for the day. I'd meet up with Marco, feed the wolves, then I'd make a little detour before lunch and drop in at Dahlia's to do a little snooping. I couldn't get around the feeling that she might be hiding something—something Rich might have confronted her about.

I wasn't sure how to finagle my way into her house, but maybe I could use the excuse that Evie wanted me to whip up another batch of lavender lemonade.

I suddenly realized that I hadn't seen Dahlia or Carson at all yesterday. Surely if they'd left town, Evie would have let us know? Besides, Sergeant Hardy would have instructed them to stick close since Rich's death was now an official homicide.

My landline rang, and I jumped. No one ever called me at my home phone. The caller ID read "Jacob Hardy."

"Hello?" My greeting was a question.

"Belinda. Sergeant Hardy here. We need to take your statement about finding Rich O'Brien. I know you were with me at the time, but obviously we have to get each witness's account recorded, and I have to turn those in today."

"Sure. Do I need to come to the police station?" I didn't mention that I'd visited the station this past winter. I had even made a detective friend in the police department—Hugh Watson. I wondered if he would be assigned to this case.

"We can meet wherever it's convenient for you. I won't be in the office today, but I'll need to stop for lunch. I think it's going to be nice out, so would you want to meet at Byram Park?"

It was a bit out of the way, and I didn't want to cut into my break time due to my self-scheduled recon mission in Dahlia's house. Also, I had no desire to be alone with Sergeant Hardy in a more secluded area like the park.

I threw out another suggestion. "How about the library? That's closer to me...although, come to think of it, you couldn't eat your lunch inside."

"That'd be fine—they have some benches outside. What time works for you?"

We agreed to meet at noon, and I hoped it wouldn't take long to rehash the events of that tragic morning. I would rather use my free time to find Rich's killer, not to talk about things that couldn't be changed.

Both Katrina and Jonas would be livid that I had decided to go on the prowl for a murderer. But someone had to get serious about this investigation, and I was not at all convinced that Sergeant Jacob Hardy was.

* * * *

When I walked into the visitors' center, Evie sat behind the front desk, deep in conversation on her cell phone. Her British accent was pronounced, and her clipped tone said she was all business. I acted like I wasn't listening, but it was clear she was considering a move...back to Britain. She appeared to be pricing flats near her parents.

By the time I deposited my lunch in the fridge and pulled on my green vest, Evie had fallen silent. I went out to say hello, and was surprised to find her patting her eyes with a tissue.

I closed the distance between us. "Evie? Are you okay?"

The striking woman turned her reddened eyes my way. "I thought I was, but then I couldn't sleep last night, even though I know I'm safe enough with the Fentons. And this morning when I parked my car, I saw movement in the woods. The officer on duty was sitting in his car the entire time, and he said he didn't see a thing. I feel like I'm going crazy. I can't live like this, Belinda. I simply can't."

All the comforting words I came up with just didn't ring true, because Evie was right. If I were in her position, I would either track my ex down using less-than-aboveboard methods, or I would leave without a trace.

I was about to murmur something sympathetic when Marco strode into the gift shop. Evie ducked behind the counter, probably trying to hide her state of dismay.

I rushed to cover for her. "Hi, Marco. Are you here to feed the wolves already? It's a little early, isn't it?"

He trudged toward the kitchen, his thick-soled boots leaving dirt clods behind. "It is, but I have to tie up a few loose ends before my trip next week, so I'll only be here for the next few mornings."

I followed him into the kitchen to help him load up. "But I'll be leaving around the same time," I said. "Who's going to feed the animals then?"

He shrugged. "I honestly don't know. Dahlia said she was going to ask Veronica, but she would need someone stronger to help her load the meats."

"Maybe Carson?" I suggested.

Marco sneered. "That boy's lucky to drag his sorry carcass out of bed in the mornings."

"He wasn't here yesterday," I mused aloud. "I know his grandpa was looking for someone to fill in at his company. Maybe Carson took him up on the job."

Marco tilted his head and gave me a long look. "You're quite a kindhearted little thing, aren't you? I don't think I've heard anyone give Carson the benefit of the doubt before, with the exception of his mother. But sure, maybe he took the job with Dennis. We can only hope."

"Do you know if Dahlia was out yesterday, as well?"

He turned to look in the meat fridge. "I don't know."

Given his evasive body language and vague answer, I didn't believe him. Maybe he was lying to hide his relationship with Dahlia. Or maybe he was covering for her for some other reason…

I shook my head, focusing on the job at hand. As I tossed meat into the buckets, I knew one thing for sure—I wasn't the kindhearted little thing Marco assumed I was.

At this stage in the game, I had begun to suspect everyone. And if Evie's ex was killing people, I wanted him to be exposed before Evie had to uproot her life and run, yet again.

Since I was a brand-new employee at the preserve, I had a little more wiggle room if someone caught me exploring in places I shouldn't.

And I planned to do just that.

22

As I poured the water in Thor's enclosure, I noticed the pack seemed disinterested in their food. I hoped this didn't mean they were sick, since I doubted Dahlia would know how to care for them. I looked closer. The wolves actually looked sleepy. Maybe they weren't morning animals.

Freya seemed content to lie near my feet, but when I turned off the spigot, she roused and gave a howl.

Immediately, the other wolves started howling, which completely freaked me out. "What's wrong?"

Marco pulled off his gloves. "If I'm not mistaken, Freya is just saying she likes you. And the rest of the pack is responding to her."

"You mean they're agreeing with her?"

Marco cocked his head, listening. "I don't speak wolf as well as Rich did, but I think they're just happy she's feeling good."

Made sense to me. I leaned down and rubbed Freya's back, thankful for what felt like the only genuine camaraderie I'd had at the preserve, saving Rich and Shaun.

Njord was quick to welcome us to his enclosure with friendly nose nudges, and the sibling wolves were full of themselves, tumbling around in the grass. I chuckled, comparing this pack's alert morning state with Thor's pack, which must be night owls.

Marco fed them so quickly, I had to linger a bit to finish filling the watering trough. I noticed that Marco wasn't nearly as friendly with Njord as Rich had been. Surely he wasn't a little afraid of the wolves? He didn't rub the wolves in this enclosure much—simply patted their heads like they were a distraction. I supposed it was possible that if Marco had been the one to transport the abused wolves to the preserve, they might associate him with memories of the dismal place they'd come from. Maybe he triggered them, so to speak.

But I also remembered what Jonas had said, that if the person who'd killed Rich hadn't understood pack dynamics, they might have assumed Njord and his pack would have chomped right into Rich. In fact, they would have been counting on it. When the wolves didn't touch Rich's body, their plan backfired. In that case, it wasn't a psychopath who'd carefully set the stage...it was someone trying to cover their tracks, someone who was basically thwarted by the wolves.

I turned off the water and looked at Marco, who was lounging by the open gate. It was far-fetched to think he would kill two people just to get Dahlia to live with him. I returned to the idea of some kind of illegal transaction. What if the wolves had been slated to be eliminated due to dangerous behavior and he'd snagged them and presented them to Dahlia as if they were on the up and up? And maybe now he had to clean up his trail by making sure the wolves had to be put down?

Njord looked at me expectantly, like he was either wishing I'd brought my friend Jonas or like he was reading my thoughts. Did he sense my unease over Marco? The way he trotted alongside me as I walked to the gate, I almost believed he did.

* * * *

Marco went home soon after we returned to the visitors' center. Evie was in the kitchen, talking on the phone as she nibbled dainty bites of some kind of blue cheese salad. Since I couldn't get her attention, I scrawled a note on a napkin saying I'd be back in an hour, and she nodded. I grabbed my lunch bag and walked out to Bluebell.

The day was beautiful, just as Sergeant Hardy had said it would be. As I drove past gated homes with trimmed hedgerows and private pools, I wondered for the hundredth time what it would be like to be a landowner in this town. Mom hadn't raised me to fixate on money—quite the opposite, in fact—but I'd seen how the other side lived in Greenwich, and it did have its allure.

My reading of *The Great Gatsby* had further fueled my delusions of grandeur. Adam and Ada had taken me in like one of their own, and they were planning several summer parties they wanted me to attend so I could mingle with their upper-crust friends. Even though I was an introvert, I knew these would be the type of small-scale, fully catered parties I'd enjoy.

I mentally shook myself. Greenwich wasn't who I *was,* no matter how friendly the Fentons, Dietrich, and the Carringtons were to me. I would always be an outsider…a poser. Like Gatsby.

I pulled into the library parking lot, glancing around for a police vehicle. When I didn't see one, I dug around in my lunch bag and withdrew a squashed turkey and Swiss sandwich and a bag of barbecue chips. Living the life of luxury, I was not.

I was halfway through my sandwich when a black car pulled up next to mine. Sergeant Hardy rolled down his window. "Sorry I was late. The drive-through took forever. Want to sit down somewhere?"

I agreed, grabbed my water bottle, and followed him to a shady bench. It felt strange sitting next to an officer in uniform, and we received more than a few stares.

"I feel like I'm with a celebrity," I joked.

Sergeant Hardy smiled, and I had to admit it went a long way toward softening his appearance. "I've learned to ignore the looks," he said.

I glanced around. The bench was visible to anyone walking by, and the library was busy today. I took my confidence in both hands and said, "Veronica told me you two are dating. Don't you think that might compromise the homicide investigation?"

His pen remained clenched in his large hand, but his expression was calm. "I don't, because I'm actually working under someone else now. A detective," he added.

"It wouldn't be Detective Watson, would it?" I always smiled when I said that name, because it reminded me of Sherlock Holmes's crime-solving partner.

Sergeant Hardy gave me a disbelieving look. "You know him?"

I took a long drink of water to slow my dramatic reveal. "I sure do."

He looked at me with fresh respect. "Detective Watson's the cream of the crop. He's determined to find out what's going on at the White Pine preserve."

I felt more comfortable knowing Detective Watson was on the case. The West Virginia native brought a down-home sensibility to his police work, and he liked to get his man.

After pushing the record button on his phone, Sergeant Hardy took notes as I walked him through what I'd seen the day we found Rich. He injected a couple of pointed questions about where Dahlia had been that morning, which I thought was strange. Did he seriously suspect the wolf preserve owner? And why?

I glanced at my phone. "I've got to get going," I said, not sharing that I intended to use the rest of my lunch break to snoop around in Dahlia's house. I was pretty sure she wasn't around today, which in itself was strange for someone whose entire business had just been turned upside down by a murder.

Or was it two murders? "Did you find out for certain if Rich or Shaun were poisoned?" I asked.

Sergeant Hardy looked off into the distance. "Now, you know I can't tell you that, Miss Blake. What would Detective Watson say if he knew I was sharing privileged information with a civilian?"

"But if someone's killing people at the preserve, don't you think the employees should know? Especially your girlfriend?" I pressed.

His dark brows lowered. "As a matter of fact, I do. I've been telling Veronica to get out of there, but she's so devoted to writing a killer thesis, she won't listen. I can't answer you directly, but I'll reiterate that it's not safe, and I'd suggest you leave as soon as possible."

So he had to be saying that one or both men were poisoned. Poisoned, dragged into the wolf enclosure, and discarded like bags of trash.

I muttered a strained good-bye to the sergeant, then walked back to my car, filled with a noble fury. Shaun had been a jovial, harmless guy. It made no sense that someone might have ruthlessly poisoned him.

And how had the poisoner gotten to his victims in the first place? Slipped something in a cup of coffee? Offered a spiked water bottle? Shot them with a poisoned blow dart?

By the time I pulled into the driveway at White Pine, I was more determined than ever to find out all I could about Dahlia. If the police were looking in that direction, well, so could I.

23

Evie was sitting next to the front window in the gift shop. Her back was stiff, like she was on high alert. She must have spent half her day in that watchful position. The patrol officer was no longer on duty, so she was basically on her own if someone burst into the visitors' center.

At least I assumed she was on her own.

"Evie, do you have any idea where Dahlia and Carson are today?"

She gave a long sigh. "To tell the truth, that's something that has always frustrated me about this job. Dahlia is prone to leaving the preserve without a moment's notice. In fact, the only reason she called you before she left to fly to Arizona was because Rich was pushing for help and I looked you up. She treats this preserve like it can run itself."

As I'd begun to realize, Rich had been spot-on when he said Dahlia wasn't involved with her wolves. She rescued them and got them to the preserve, yes—but not much more.

"So you don't know where she is?"

"The last time I saw her was yesterday evening, when she was talking with Marco." She fell strangely silent.

"I know they're together," I said.

She arched an eyebrow. "You're terribly observant, aren't you? I'm impressed, because they've kept it quite secret. You *are* right about them, but last night it sounded as if they had a bit of a row."

"Do you think she took off somewhere?"

"I don't know."

It was exactly the same answer Marco had given me, but I actually believed Evie. She was obviously irritated.

"I've tried calling her mobile so many times," Evie continued. "I've gone over to the house, and she wasn't there. I need to get her approval on some paperwork."

"But what about Carson? Where's he?"

"That's another good question. I know for certain he was here last night, because he had nearly every light in the house blazing. It's his habit—he seems to have no concept of electric bills," she complained. "Anyway, this morning, when you were out with Marco, someone did drop by, looking for Carson. He was the same man I'd seen here a couple of months ago."

"A return tourist?" I guessed.

She shook her head. "No, and quite frankly, I was surprised to see him again. The last time he was here, he drove some large piece of equipment out into the woods—it looked like it had a drill on it. I think Carson said he'd gone up by some caves. Afterward, when he met up with Carson in the visitors' center, I overheard the man saying he'd hit dirt. I assumed that meant whatever he was drilling for was a bust."

Had Carson or Dahlia paid someone to drill for something? Natural gas? Surely not oil, in this area? Regardless, it sounded like the driller didn't hit anything of importance.

"What did the man want today?" I asked.

"He headed over to Dahlia's house, so I don't know what he wanted. He refused to leave a number." Evie's voice was growing more testy by the minute. "I can't continue running this place on my own. Do you know who keeps the meat and vitamins ordered for the wolves and the barnyard animals? I do. Do you know who cuts all the paychecks? I do."

I knew Evie was overwhelmed with worry over her ex, and Dahlia was only adding to it with her daily desertions. "Thanks so much, Evie—I know it must be frustrating. Do you want me to check next door again and see if anyone's home?"

Evie dropped into her chair, pulling a key from her pocket and offering it to me. "Would you? That would be so helpful. Here's the house key—ring the bell, but if no one answers, go in and call for Dahlia. These papers are coming due soon."

"Will do," I said, trying not to smile. Evie had just given me the perfect excuse for rummaging around in Dahlia's house. As I turned to leave, I realized there was one final obstacle to my well-laid plans.

"By the way, where's Veronica today?" I asked, as casually as I could.

"She called in with a bad cold," Evie said. "She said she hopes to be back tomorrow, although she does sound horrible."

That meant I'd be feeding the smaller animals myself, but I'd gotten the routine down pretty smoothly, as long as there wasn't another raccoon rampage.

"That's too bad. I'll see you in a bit." I shut the wooden door behind me and walked up the path to Dahlia's house. I kept a steady stride, as if I were just a normal employee looking for her employer. Nothing to see here, folks.

I held my breath and rang her doorbell. If she was home, I'd simply deliver Evie's message, then beat a hasty retreat. If Dahlia was the killer, she'd definitely get suspicious if I started asking if she'd met with Rich at The Apricot Macaron.

I waited for about twenty slow seconds, then rang the bell again. When no one answered the second time, I used the key and opened the door. To be on the safe side, I yelled for Dahlia several times and got no reply. I figured Carson wasn't home, either, since he surely would have heard the doorbell or my shouts.

I didn't have to guess where Dahlia's office was, because she had a very girlie-looking nook set up in the corner of her living room. A computer, a printer, and several hanging files sat on an ivory and pink desk that could not possibly belong to Carson, unless I'd totally misjudged him.

I edged that way, glanced around, then slid behind the desk to read the file names. *Njord, Freya, Thor, Saga*...there was a file for each wolf.

I picked up Thor's file and perused it. Several photos of him looking emaciated were clipped to the inside, and I assumed they had been taken before he was brought here. Marco had typed up a couple of reports that detailed Thor's date of birth, his weight, and his registration chip number. None of the information conflicted, so it appeared that everything had been done according to procedure.

I slid Thor's file back into the holder. Stepping into the middle of the living room, I shouted again. "Dahlia?"

Again, there was no response, but I had the strange feeling that someone was watching me. I hesitated a moment or two, then, convinced I was imagining things, I scooted back to my position behind the desk and started pulling drawers open. I rifled around, but found nothing mysterious in them—and nothing vaguely business-related, either. They were stuffed with beauty products like nail polish and lotions.

I gave a snort. Despite her hassled and unkempt appearance, Dahlia was a beauty product hoarder. I never would've guessed.

When I shifted the mouse for her computer, a screensaver image popped up—a photo of Dahlia and Marco on the beach. Looking closer, I realized it wasn't taken at some exotic locale, but at the local Greenwich beach.

The computer was password-protected, and I knew my hacking game wasn't strong, at least compared to that of some of my gamer friends. It seemed as if my risk-taking hadn't been worth it.

I was just about to open the front door when the knob turned and I found myself face-to-face with Dahlia herself. She wore an oversized men's shirt, and her hair was thrown up into a large, side-tilted clip on top of her head.

"Belinda?" she asked, obviously stunned to see me standing in her living room.

I maintained my façade, feigning irritation. "I was looking for you— Evie sent me over. I've been yelling and yelling."

Dahlia slid her keys into her purse. "Well, I've been out. She should have called."

"She said she did. Numerous times. She has some urgent papers she needs you to sign."

Dahlia was just as unprepared for my accusatory tone as I'd been for her to walk through that door. She stammered, "Yes, well, of course, I'll drop over at the visitors' center as soon as I can. Please let Evie know that I have to eat my lunch first, but then I'll come right over."

I nodded and stepped around her. "I'll do that. Thanks, Dahlia."

She still wore a bewildered look when I closed the front door behind me. But I wasn't in the dark anymore. As I'd passed by Dahlia, I'd caught a whiff of cologne, and I was pretty sure it was Marco's.

All the signs pointed to the possibility that Dahlia had made up with Marco last night, then stayed over at his house. She probably hadn't bothered to check her phone while she was there.

I strode over to the visitors' center to give Evie the scoop. While I couldn't write Dahlia off as a suspect, I felt like the biggest thing she was hiding was her relationship with Marco.

As I approached the visitors' center, I nearly careened into Dennis Arden, who was striding vigorously toward Dahlia's house. He stopped and gave me an apologetic look.

"Sorry for almost plowing you down there. I heard that Dahlia's still upset about the newspaper reports, so I brought her a piece of coffee cake—it's Madeline's recipe. I make it about once every month or so, just to remember her, and it struck me that Dahlia might enjoy it, too."

I felt like he was laying it on thick—both his loyalty to his dead wife and his attempt to do something nice for Dahlia, but maybe he'd turned a corner.

"That's thoughtful," I said.

He peered at me. "Has anyone ever told you that you look a little like Marjorie Reynolds?"

I gave him a blank look and he elaborated. "She was an actress in *Holiday Inn* with Bing Crosby—she played Linda Mason. She had the same fresh charm you have."

I knew a come-on when I heard it, even when it popped out of the lips of an old widower.

"Nope, no one has ever told me that." I didn't stick around to let him further elaborate on my looks. Instead, I made a beeline for the side door of the visitors' center. I hurried through the kitchen and into the gift shop.

Evie was still positioned by the window. I couldn't believe she wasn't even scrolling around on her phone—her gaze was fixed on the parking lot. The poor woman was terrified. It was no way to live.

She briefly turned my way. "Did you find Dahlia?"

"Actually, I did. She just got back—probably from Marco's. She said she's going to grab lunch and then come over to sign your papers."

"Perfect. Thanks heaps for handling that for me." Evie took a deep breath and stood. She motioned me over to a display table. "One quick question—do you think these mugs are tacky or simply unusual? They just came in today."

The mugs featured watercolor wolves painted in sherbet colors. The paint softened into streaks at their necks and seemed to run down the bottom portion of the mug.

"I think they're unusual," I said, trying to be polite. "I'm sure they'll appeal to some people."

"Thanks," she said. "What do you have left today?"

"I just have to feed the goats, peacocks, and chickens," I said. "And now that the grass has thickened up, the goats don't need as much feed."

"Sounds good. I'll see you in a bit, then." Evie turned back to the table, rearranging the painted mugs so they were more visible.

Katrina would say Evie's sudden need to perfect the display table was an avoidance tactic, something to give her a reprieve from thinking about the possible proximity of her stalker ex.

Katrina would be right.

Determined to help Evie any way I could, I headed out the kitchen door, but instead of going to do my chores, I circled the barn and crept into the woods by the parking lot. After slipping my pepper spray into my right hand, I slid my cell phone into my left. If Evie's ex, Brian, was hanging out where he had been the last time, I could startle him, then call the cops.

But as I closed in on the bramble hedges he'd skulked around in last time, it was obvious no one was there. Disappointed that I couldn't bust the creeper, I scanned the ground and bushes for evidence he had returned, but there was none.

Pocketing my spray and phone, I headed back to the red building to grab the chicken feed. On my way to the coop, I caught a glimpse of Dennis, who was hustling down the pathway from Dahlia's. He acted like he was anxious to leave the preserve, but he didn't veer off toward the parking lot.

Instead, he headed toward the woods.

Why would he be going that direction? As far as I knew, he'd never been friendly with the wolves. Unless he planned to take a relaxing stroll, he had no reason to take that route.

But he hadn't been strolling.

Absently, I scattered chicken feed and glanced at the patched hole in the fence. The raccoon must have sworn off his breaking-and-entering ways, since the mended wire still looked untouched.

The small-brained chickens wouldn't have known what hit them, had Jonas not intervened in time. I'd seen raccoons in action in my mom's coop before, and they were *not* the kind of animals that backed down. It surprised me that Jonas's stick techniques had even worked, but then again, the raccoon hadn't made much headway into the coop when Veronica had found him.

As the hens pecked about contentedly, my thoughts drifted once again to Shaun. Did the poison hit him suddenly, making him drop to the ground? Did someone spring from the trees and drag Shaun's rigid body into Njord's enclosure? They'd have to be considerably strong, given that Shaun had looked to be over two hundred fifty pounds.

And then Rich...assuming he was the one who'd met Dahlia at The Apricot Macaron, he had argued with her—about what? Was Rich going to blow the whistle on Dahlia somehow? Or was he simply sick of her taking all the credit for his work with the wolves? Why would he feel the need to meet her publicly, instead of just talking with her on the preserve?

And what linked Shaun and Rich together that made them both threats to someone? There had to be a link...unless they were simply random victims chosen by a psychopath, as Katrina had suggested.

Yet, didn't the fact that both victims were dragged into the wolf enclosures mean that someone had intended to pin their deaths on the wolves? That would point to someone trying to take down the entire wolf preserve.

I shook my head, feeling like I'd come full circle. I still knew next to nothing about the murderer.

I'd finished with the peacocks and was starting to water the goats when I realized Dahlia still hadn't emerged from her house. A queasy feeling hit my stomach as I pictured Dennis, walking so purposefully toward Dahlia's house...and then away from it.

He had delivered a piece of coffee cake. *One* piece. Made specifically for Dahlia.

Alarm spread through me like a fever and I shoved past goats to jump the fence. I ran toward Dahlia's and rang her bell. When there was no answer, I impatiently banged on the door several times. In the dead silence that ensued, I tried the doorknob, but it was locked.

I bolted back to the visitors' center, charging through the kitchen door. I didn't see Evie anywhere, so I gave a few loud shouts. She opened the front door and poked her head in, a watering can in hand and an anxious look on her face.

"What's going on?" she asked.

I tried to catch my breath. "Evie, you have to call Sergeant Hardy. I think Dahlia might have been poisoned," I said. "Was Dennis in here today?"

"He was here earlier, yes."

"Did you notice if he took the new key to Njord's enclosure? Or is it still hanging in the kitchen?"

"He went into the kitchen briefly—said he had some kind of food for Dahlia. That's all I know."

I couldn't stand around talking anymore. "Call the sergeant, then use your key and check on Dahlia!" I commanded. "I'm heading to the woods."

As Evie withdrew her phone, I scuttled past her and jogged into the woods. I felt for my pepper spray, then pulled it out as I neared Thor's enclosure. My phone was in my vest pocket, backup in case things went south.

I figured I'd have the drop on Dennis, since he wouldn't be expecting me. And he was older, so I had the advantage. He was definitely taller than I was, but I had no doubt I could move faster.

I tried to process my racing thoughts. Had Dennis hated Dahlia's wolf preserve so much, he'd been willing to murder so it would be pinned on the wolves? Or had he wanted his property back? After all, a parcel of wooded land this large would command a small fortune in Greenwich. Or maybe he wasn't going to sell at all—maybe he'd planned to build a day spa here, to fulfill his wife's dream.

I glanced around Thor's enclosure, and nothing seemed to be moving, not even the wolves. As I got closer, I could see they were napping. Thor's pack certainly seemed to be more tired in the daytime than Njord's.

The metal pepper spray canister slipped a bit, and I repositioned my fingers. The day was mild, but my internal temperature had somehow spiked and I was sweating. Katrina would say I was in fight-or-flight mode, and she'd be right.

Today, I had chosen *fight*.

24

Njord sat in the grass, a long patch of white in a sea of green, as I approached the first gate of his enclosure. I glanced over my shoulder no fewer than ten times as I examined the locks, but they didn't seem to be open.

Saga and Siggie trotted past, giving me curious looks. None of the wolves seemed overly excited or upset, so I had to assume that nothing unusual had occurred today.

I turned my back to them, slowly running my gaze over each tree. A cardinal sat warbling on a nearby limb, as if nothing was amiss.

I supposed Dennis could have taken the loop through the woods and come out by the parking lot before I saw him. Maybe he really had just been taking a brisk walk on the property. Had I jumped to conclusions?

I knew I should head back to check on Dahlia, but something was bothering me. What had Evie said about the man who'd come to drill—that he'd been working near some caves in the woods?

I vaguely recalled seeing a stony area some distance from the trail when Shaun had taken me on that first tour. I struck off in that direction. If nothing else, I might uncover something about what type of drilling had been done there.

Had someone approached Dahlia about drilling for natural gas or oil on her property? She would have likely jumped at the possibility for more income. What if the drillers had originally said nothing was there, but when they examined a sample, they had discovered there was?

Maybe that's why the driller had returned today—to tell the Whites they were going to be rich.

If Carson knew about the drilling and had let the possibility of fossil fuels slip to his grandfather, Dennis would have had an even stronger motive to get his property back, so he could control the fortune in the ground. Once Dahlia was out of the way, Dennis's son, Quinn, would have likely returned the land to his father if he'd asked for it—especially in memory of his late mother...

I rounded a corner where wide, flat rocks formed a hill. Heavy machinery had torn deep tracks in the forest floor, and they led straight to the rocky area. I followed the dirt grooves and broken twigs straight to the rock facing. It looked solid—there were only cracks for snakes to slide under, and luckily snakes weren't a big problem around here.

The trail seemed to curve around the side of the hill, so I took a shortcut and climbed up the overhang. When I looked over, it was obvious there was no solid rock wall in the back—in fact, it looked like a wide-open space. So there *was* a cave here.

Backtracking down the hill, I took the long way around the rocky outcropping. As the cave came into view, so did something else.

A man, standing on the leaf-strewn ground in front of the cave. He stopped and looked directly at me, and I let out a relieved breath when I realized it was only Carson.

* * * *

"I thought I heard someone rustling around up there," Carson said.

I didn't have time for small talk. "Have you seen your grandpa?" I asked. If Dennis had already poisoned Dahlia, it was entirely possible he'd try to take out Carson, as well. Especially if Carson was next in line for his property.

Carson gave me a strange look. "As a matter of fact, I have. Just a little bit ago, I saw him rush out to the woods, so I followed him—secretly, of course—and he headed straight for this cave. He went inside, and I followed him a little way. He had one of those lantern flashlights, but I couldn't see enough to put one foot in front of the other, so I came back out."

I clenched my pepper spray. "It's a good thing you didn't follow him any farther—he could be dangerous."

"What do you mean, *dangerous*?"

"Just a suspicion I'm following up on," I said. I squinted, trying to see into the darkened cave. When my eyes adjusted, I could make out some dim light emanating from the interior.

"Okay." I glanced back at him. "Do you have a phone on you?"

"No," he said, shrugging. "I'd just gotten home when I saw Gramps heading into the woods. I left my phone in the car and followed him."

"Okay. Just use my phone." I handed it to him, punching in the unlock code. "You need to call the cops and explain where this cave is located."

Carson looked nervous. "I'll call them, but what are you going to do?"

"I'm just going to get a little closer, see if I can see what he's up to." I opened my palm, showing him the pepper spray. "Don't worry, I'm armed."

"But what if he has a weapon, too?"

"I'm not going to get that close," I said. "But I'll give a shout if I get in trouble, and then you could come and help me." Although recalling his wailing shenanigans, I fully expected him to hightail it the opposite direction if I started yelling.

He pushed his glasses up. "Okay," he said hesitantly.

I turned back to the cave, rolling my eyes. I could see why Carson frustrated everyone around him. He wasn't exactly the kind of capable backup I would choose.

Counting on the element of surprise to help me, I gripped the spray and crept inside. I waited until my eyes adjusted, then silently moved toward the light.

Had Dennis come all the way out here just to check the drill site? Or was he preparing to kill someone else? Was this his lair, the place he'd lurked before attacking Shaun and Rich?

I was surprised at how large the cave was. As it angled downhill, I inched forward, sliding my hands along the damp wall. The walls widened into an round, open area. A battery-run lantern was positioned in the middle of the floor, throwing light on several jars of dirt sitting near the wall. Other than that, the area appeared empty.

Walking toward the jars, I tripped into something large and dark. Biting back a scream, I jumped over it and raced toward the lantern. I snatched it up and swung it around to illuminate what I'd tripped over.

It was a body.

It looked like Dennis. His eyes were closed, and he almost seemed to be napping.

Was he pretending to be hurt or dead, just to get me closer? That would be a very psychopathic thing to do.

I extended the lantern, slowly moving toward him. His eyelids didn't flutter, and in the flickering light, I couldn't tell if he was breathing or not. I didn't want to get close enough to feel for a pulse, because this felt like a trap.

Three short claps sounded from behind Dennis, and Carson came into view. He pointed my cell phone flashlight directly at me. I had to shield my eyes so its intense beam didn't blind me.

"Thanks for the light—all the better to see you with," he said. His voice was filled with a threatening surety I never would have dreamed he possessed. "Belinda, Belinda. You should've left well enough alone."

I was an idiot. How had I not seen this?

"But the wolves…they chewed you…" I struggled to make sense of things.

He laughed. "They'll chew on anything that smells like meat if you shove it in their stupid mouths. I figured my attack would throw everyone off, and it worked."

I had to admit he was right. Carson was far more devious than anyone could have guessed. I glanced down at Dennis, who still wasn't moving. "But why kill your grandpa? What did he have to do with anything?"

He seemed eager to explain, like a little boy who was proud of his science project. "Gramps was in my way. Mom was well in hand—she was gearing up to close the preserve because the unfortunate wolf attacks had *so* maligned her good name. But since Gramps rightly owned the land, I figured I'd have to get rid of him, too. I told him to meet me here so we could talk about convincing Mom to shut the preserve. He never imagined he was going to become wolf attack victim number three."

"So you poisoned him, too? But how?"

"But, but, but—you're full of questions, aren't you?" He casually leaned against the rock wall, and I saw my chance.

Springing toward the now-unblocked exit, I tried to shove past Carson. I aimed the pepper spray at his face and pressed the button, but it only gave a light hiss, and nothing came out. At the same time, something hit my stomach with a thud that reverberated throughout my body. I crumpled to the floor, the wind knocked out of me. My grip on the worthless pepper spray loosened, and it rolled some distance away.

He loomed toward me, holding a wooden two-by-four. Shaking his head, he crouched nearby. "No one thinks of checking the pepper sprays." He chuckled. "I made sure they were all empty. Still, I wish you hadn't gone and done that." He reached over and touched a curl that dangled in front of my eyes, his voice softening. "You want to know the truth? You're far hotter than Veronica. I had no real interest in her, you understand. She was a nuisance, someone I had to attach myself to so I could keep her away from the cave. She's the only one who tended to wander in the woods."

Everything swirled into crystal-clear focus. That's why Carson was always trailing Veronica around—to keep tabs on her. Yet he'd fooled everyone into thinking he was her lovesick admirer.

My face must have registered my surprise, because he gave me a wicked grin. "I'm not the idiot everyone took me for—my own mother didn't even believe in me. But guess what? I've used my geology degree to find the mother lode on this property—no one else could've done that."

"Natural gas, was it?" I asked, gingerly propping myself up on one elbow.

Keeping his grip on the board, he grabbed one of the glass jars from the floor. "No—this."

All I could see was dirt. "Is it gold?" I asked.

"In Greenwich? Of course not. This is rare earth element. I found a massive cluster of it in this cave."

I couldn't hide my bewildered look. "Earth element? You mean dirt?"

"No—it's a term for special metal elements that are used in most technological devices, like those computers and game systems you're so fond of." He actually had the gall to wink at me before continuing his explanation. "Rare earths are in constant demand. Usually, the deposits occur in very small quantities, and rarely in the United States. But we have a large cluster of the stuff, so I'm going to make a sweet fortune—after I get my hands on Grandpa's property."

My stomach muscles felt battered, and I knew they were going to bruise. Maybe if I kept Carson talking, he'd be distracted so I could attempt another run for the outside.

Then again, maybe he'd wallop me in the head with that board.

As usual, I found myself wondering what Katrina would do in this situation—how would she deal with Carson? He was obviously unhinged—who else would kill his own grandpa?

Psychopaths liked killing and they were even proud of it, Katrina had said. I needed to get him talking about his murders.

"Why'd you kill Shaun and Rich?" I straightened into a sitting position, hoping I could get to my feet quickly if given the opportunity. "And how?"

"It's a long story, but I guess we have time for it, since no one has a clue where we are." Smiling, he set the board down. Hope rose in my chest.

Then he extracted a hypodermic syringe from his jeans pocket.

He began to explain. "This is how. It's a potent dose of my mom's wolf tranquilizers. I thought those bumbling cops would figure it out earlier in the investigation and nail Mom to the wall, but they're so behind the curve."

The perfect setup. If he didn't shut his mom down with the feigned wolf attacks, he would have done it with the tranquilizer overdoses.

He went on. "I paid Rich to let me feed the wolves for several days. See, I knew that Rich was underpaid—and I knew he'd tried to butter Mom up by taking her to some fancy café to ask for a raise. His plan totally backfired, because she outright refused him. Mom isn't the best boss, as you might have figured out. Anyway, as anyone would have expected, Rich threatened to quit."

He crouched near me, the needle still in hand, as he continued. "But I got to him first. I gave him a sob story about how my mom didn't even trust me to feed the wolves, and I just wanted a chance to do it. Then I offered him money, and that swayed our desperate father of the bride. He made a show of wheeling the food into the woods, but then he'd leave it for me to distribute. What he didn't know was that I was burying it out in the woods, so the wolves went hungry."

Carson had been laying his plans for a while, then. "Why did you kill Shaun?" I asked. "I can't imagine he was any threat to you."

"He had overheard me talking on the phone with one of my professors about rare earth, right after the drilling. He started asking questions. Knowing how he practically worshiped my mom, it was only a matter of time before he put two and two together and told her she might be sitting on a fortune. Or he could have eventually blackmailed me. I couldn't let either of those things happen."

I put my hand on my stomach because it was killing me. "So you starved the wolves. Then you gave Shaun a shot of tranquilizer, and dragged him into Njord's enclosure?"

"I smeared meat on him first, then when I dropped him in there, I held up his hand for the wolves to smell. Didn't take long until they were going to town."

I cringed as the unwelcome visual sprang to mind. "And Rich...he'd started figuring things out, hadn't he? He kept telling the police the wolves shouldn't have been that hungry."

Carson nodded. "I thought about paying him more to keep his mouth shut, but I knew he could try to soak me for the rest of my life. He was easy enough to kill since he was always out in the woods, but then those idiot wolves wouldn't even touch him. And Sergeant Hardy happened to be hanging around that day, so he messed things up by getting to him faster than I'd expected."

I glanced around, my hopes dwindling. Carson was right—no one had any idea I'd wandered out to this cave. If he gave me that poisoned shot, I'd be dead before I was found.

Survival instinct kicked in. I had to get out of the cave at any cost.

I had one chance to escape, and I couldn't afford to miscalculate. Something told me that if I tried to make a break for it from my seated position, he'd have that needle jammed into me before I got off the ground.

An idea presented itself to me. Katrina had a surefire method for getting me to do what she wanted—she used reverse psychology. It was a long shot, but maybe that would work on Carson.

I feigned a shiver. "I know you're going to kill me," I said, allowing my voice to quake. "But please don't take me to the wolves. I can't handle the idea of getting eaten by them. It's just inhumane."

Carson didn't answer right away. If he was a true psychopath, he'd probably relish my fear and try to capitalize on it.

A small smile played at his lips, and he touched my leg. I tried not to recoil.

"Are you begging me?" he asked.

I hated degrading myself like this, but I did it anyway. "Yes," I squeaked.

He leaned in closer, small teeth glistening in the light like a feral animal's. His voice was cajoling. "I hate to tell you, but this was the fate I'd already decided for you. 'Such a beautiful face,' they'll say. 'So innocent. She didn't deserve to die this way.'" He seemed to perk up. "I can imagine the headlines now. It'll be the final nail in Mom's coffin—so to speak."

Pulling twine out of his pocket, he forced me to stand, then tied my wrists together behind my back. The twine was somewhat frayed, and I wondered if I could finagle my way out of it at some point.

He held the needle at my back like it was a loaded gun. "Now, walk," he commanded. He grabbed the lantern and held it aloft, so I stumbled forward. When we reached the fresh outdoor air, I gulped some in and kept moving. We trudged around the outcropping and toward the main path.

"Don't think anyone's coming for you," he said. "Mom's probably in the visitors' center with Evie, and Veronica's not here today. Marco already left, as you're probably aware."

At least Carson spoke of his mother in the present tense, so that meant he hadn't killed her yet. Maybe, in the end, she could salvage what was left of her preserve, or at least sell the wolves to someone who'd care for them.

Carson continued talking. "When you were in our house, I was waiting to see if you pulled out that last file. It was a report from the drilling company that Mom insisted on keeping. She bought my story that they'd approached me, looking for natural gas, and that they didn't find any. But their report actually specified that they were hunting for rare earth. Mom never even glanced over it—I knew she wouldn't."

Chills ran through me. So someone *had* been watching me in that house.

"I have to say, I was surprised you didn't hack into her computer. Her password's so easy: *Marco.* I mean, seriously, it's so sappy." He pulled up short as we got close to Njord's enclosure.

I was grasping at straws to divert his focus from the murder at hand. "I heard you do computer work? Do you know how to hack?"

He laughed, pulling a key from his pocket and unlocking the first gate. "Do I know how to hack? Let's just say that for about a week, every time the curvaceous Greenwich librarian Carly Browning would scan a book for checkout, 'Girls Just Want to Have Fun' blasted on the speakers."

It was funny, but I couldn't even force a laugh. I was about to have a poisoned needle plunged into my back.

I'd heard that desperation could make people do funny things, and it turned out to be true. Njord, Saga, and Siggie had all gathered close to the second gate—almost like they knew I was in trouble. For one moment, I felt like I wasn't alone.

Sergeant Hardy couldn't be far away, if Evie had indeed called him. But she might not have called him if Dahlia had shown up to sign the papers.

It was up to me. I had one chance to draw attention to myself.

I knew just how to do it.

Taking a long step that placed me a couple of inches farther from Carson, I breathed deep, then gave a long, mad wolf howl.

The wolves didn't hesitate. They picked up the chorus and added their own unique notes. Their howling filled the air, and even Thor's pack began to join in.

"Why'd you have to do that?" Carson's anger was palpable. I raced away from him, but he was lighter on his feet than I expected, and he pinned me to the ground.

As the wolves added yips to their song, I gritted my teeth, waiting for the pinch of a needle in my back.

But instead, I heard Sergeant Hardy bellow, "Get your hands in the air!"

There was a moment of loaded silence, but thankfully, Carson must have decided it wasn't worth it to kill me right in front of a police officer. He slowly climbed off me and stood to his feet. I stayed on the cool ground, my face pressed into the leafy path, my hands still tied behind my back. All my muscles were shaking, and I didn't have the strength to budge.

A police officer made his way to me and cut the twine. He helped me to my feet, asking if I was okay, but I didn't need his ministrations. Instead, I directed him toward the cave and told him to call an ambulance for Dennis, just in case it wasn't too late for him.

I bobbed on my feet as an officer handcuffed Carson and led him away, but not before the deranged killer turned and gave me a slow, lurid smile.

I was relieved when Sergeant Hardy approached me. "You did the right thing, calling me in. Dahlia's okay, by the way. She must have been showering when you tried to check on her, because she showed up at the visitors' center not long after Evie called me. I decided to trek around a bit anyway, since you were nowhere in sight."

I placed my shaky hand on his arm. "Thank goodness you did. I was one false move away from getting a heavy dose of wolf tranquilizers. That's what he's been using."

"The tox lab confirmed that this morning, but I assumed the poisoning method pointed to Dahlia. I was actually coming here to pick her up for more questioning."

I nodded. "That's exactly what Carson wanted you to think. He wanted his mom off the preserve so he could have this land to himself. There's some kind of valuable metal element he's found on the property—something worth a lot of money."

"That explains a lot. How about if you head back to the visitors' center and I'll catch up with you later, after you've had a little time to rest? Can you get back there on your own?"

I breathed deeply. My trembling seemed to have subsided. I rubbed at my wrists. "I'm okay. I'm just glad this is over."

Before I headed down the path, I walked over toward the wolf enclosure and murmured to Njord, whose eyes were fixed on me with a kind of benevolent wisdom. "You did great today," I said. "Rich would've been so proud of you."

Swiping at tears, I turned and walked away. It was time for me to find a new job.

25

I waited with Evie and a totally hysterical Dahlia as Carson was escorted off to jail and Dennis Arden was retrieved from the cave. When the paramedics flipped the siren once they'd transferred Dennis into the ambulance, I realized he might still have a chance at survival.

By the time Sergeant Hardy moseyed back to the visitors' center, I was sipping on warm chamomile tea and sitting in the only recliner in the gift shop. Evie had wrapped a quilt around me, and I'd finally stopped shaking.

The tall sergeant strode right over to me and handed me my cell phone. "He said this was yours. Also, they just told me that Dennis might make it, thanks to you, Belinda."

Evie surreptitiously handed me a packaged antibacterial wipe, which I tore into, using one to clean my phone with a righteous fury. I couldn't bear to think of that crazy killer holding on to it. Meanwhile Dahlia, who had sagged into a nearby chair, didn't say a word.

"I've called Marco," Evie whispered behind her hand. "He'll be here soon. This has all been too much for her."

Evie cast a contrite glance at Dahlia, and I knew she probably still intended to quit, just like I did. Yet our departures shouldn't come as a complete surprise to Dahlia.

I wondered if Veronica would stick around.

"Dahlia's ex is going to hire a lawyer for Carson," Evie said. "It's the least he could do, so she'll have one less thing to worry about in the aftermath of everything."

It was a relief to see Quinn stepping up for Dahlia, whose dream of owning a wolf preserve had been so hard-battered.

But at the same time, I hoped the lawyer failed miserably and Carson got the harshest sentence possible. He was the type of person who should never be allowed to be free again.

He needed to live in a cage, just like the wolves he'd tried pin his crimes on.

* * * *

When Marco arrived at the gift shop, Dahlia seemed to perk up a bit. And once Sergeant Hardy reported that the hospital said that Dennis was expected to make a full, albeit slow, recovery, Dahlia grew visibly calmer. She had probably never anticipated a day she would worry over her father-in-law's health, but today turned out to be that day.

Relieved that things seemed to be working out, I gathered my courage and approached Dahlia.

She turned watery eyes toward me. "Yes?"

Marco held her pale hand in his grip. He seemed to know what was coming next, but he gave me an encouraging nod.

"I'm leaving before the end of my contract," I said. "I'm sure you can understand." *Given that your son tried to kill me and I'll probably have traumatic flashbacks about his creepy stalker eyes following me for the rest of my life.*

"S-sure." Taking it better than I thought she would, she turned to Evie. "Dear, would you mind writing the check for Belinda?"

Evie bustled about, probably grateful for something to do. I pocketed the check she presented to me, then I offered Dahlia a weak smile. "Thank you for this opportunity. Would you mind if Marco took me back to the enclosures, so I can say a proper good-bye to the wolves?"

"Feel free." Dahlia released Marco's hand so he could join me.

Marco took my arm and steered me toward the door. Once we were outside the building, he stopped and said, "She'll be okay. It's been a shock, but she's going to pull through. I've been thinking that we might be able to spin this with the reporters—maybe say something about how the real animal at the preserve wasn't a wolf."

I felt that was a great idea for the headlines, and I said so as we walked into the woods. "But what about hired help? I probably won't be the only one leaving," I said. "Do you really think Dahlia can keep this place in operation?"

He nodded. "I think she can, if I can pick up the slack for a while. I've already canceled my trip so I can keep feeding the wolves. And although

Evie's shared that she's planning to move back to England, she just agreed to stick around until Dahlia finds someone to replace her."

"That's kind of her." Kinder than anyone knew, given Evie's on-the-loose stalker ex. I took a long look at the concerned, sturdy man next to me. "You know, Dahlia's lucky to have someone like you in her life."

Unlocking the first gate at Thor's enclosure, he turned back to me with a steady gaze. "Dahlia is a hard one to pin down. I don't know if she's interested in remarrying, but I am ready to propose."

I wasn't sure whether to congratulate him or offer condolences, given Dahlia's apparent inability to take a hands-on approach to her own wolf preserve. I offered him a quick smile, then turned to Freya. The brown wolf was prancing around and yipping sporadically, like she somehow knew this day was significant.

As soon as I got into the fence, I wordlessly knelt and ran my fingers through the soft plume of hair under her chin. When she watched me with those kind, wild eyes, I knew I'd have to return and see her again. And I'd do my part to make sure the preserve didn't have to close and leave her homeless.

Veronica had given me her number, so I decided to call and tell her about Carson as Marco led me toward Njord's enclosure. When I tapped in my phone code, a new screensaver popped up—one written in bloodred lettering.

It said: *It was a pleasure to kill you, Belinda Blake.*

I dropped my phone like it was a hot potato. Marco glanced back at me, and I tried to talk myself down as I bent to pick it up. Carson had assumed he was heading into the cave to kill me. He wrote that as a joke to himself, or to the police, I suppose.

I didn't find it very funny.

As Marco opened the first gate, I pulled it together enough to pocket my phone and follow him inside.

Njord loped right over to greet us. For the first time since I'd been at the preserve, I leaned down to rub Njord's white stomach without one iota of reservation.

Marco joined me, giving Njord's ears a vigorous petting. It was obvious that he was feeling the same sense of relief I was, now that we knew the wolves weren't vicious human-killers.

When I stood, I wobbled a bit, and Marco noticed. He took my elbow. "I'll walk you back," he said firmly. Normally, I would've protested, but given that my muscles seemed to have gone rogue, I accepted.

When we arrived at the visitors' center, Marco pulled out a chair for me because I was shaking again. Had Carson actually injected me with some of the tranquilizer? I hadn't felt anything. Surely if he'd done that, I'd be out cold.

Uncertain if I should be driving, I phoned Red. Our conversation was brief. The minute I asked if he could pick me up at the wolf preserve, he replied, "I'm on my way," and hung up.

"You okay?" Marco asked.

I nodded. "I will be. You check on Dahlia—she needs you more than I do."

Marco headed over to the white house to join Dahlia, and Evie sat down next to me. She said nothing, and I was grateful for the silence.

It didn't take long before Red pulled up and texted that he had arrived.

Evie stood, extending her hand. "Let me walk you to the car," she said.

Afraid my legs would go wobbly again, I nodded. I leaned into Evie as we walked, thankful for her instinctual kind of thoughtfulness.

Red greeted us and took my arm, leading me to the open back door of the car. There was a sudden scuffling behind him.

Evie shouted, "No!"

Red and I wheeled around, only to see that Evie's ex-husband had grabbed her and was holding a knife to her throat.

"You're coming with me," Brian said, nearly picking her off the ground. He glared at Red, then at me. "Don't take another step, or I'll slash her skinny throat, I swear."

Red gave a brief nod of surrender and raised his hands. I followed his lead, backing up and sinking into the car seat.

"You know I could never forget you," Brian O'Callaghan said, turning back to Evie. He gave her a wet kiss on her face, and I knew she was trying not to cringe.

"There's no need for the knife," Evie said. "I'll go with you peaceably, Brian."

The man blinked rapidly, as if surprised. "You would?"

Evie nodded, but the hectic pink flush on her pale cheeks belied the honesty of her statement.

Brian took a step backward, dragging Evie along with him. He took another step backward but stumbled, and the knife blade jutted toward Evie's face for one heart-stopping moment.

"Put the knife down," Evie repeated. "Otherwise you might hurt me."

Taking a glance at Red, who was still standing with his hands in the air, Brian wrapped his knife arm around Evie's waist, so the blade lay flat against her stomach. After a few more hesitant steps backward, he turned to see where he was.

In that split second, Red pulled his gun from an ankle holster, aimed, and shot—right at Brian's head.

The man's knife clattered to the ground just before he fell into a heap behind Evie. Letting out a piercing scream, Evie ran toward us, hands flailing.

By this time, Marco and Dahlia had made their way into the parking lot and stood, dumbfounded, as Red charged the fallen man, pinning him to the ground. Although there was a little blood on Brian's head, he struggled to break free of Red's weight.

"He was going to kill me. I know he was." Evie began to weep.

Finally grasping the situation, Marco rushed over to help Red subdue the writhing man on the ground. The loyal chauffeur-bodyguard shouted, "Call the cops!"

And I did just that.

* * * *

"Turns out it was just a flesh wound," Sergeant Hardy reported. "Brian got lucky, given Red's army experience. But it was a tight shot, anyone would agree. It was a good thing Red took his opportunity."

Evie sat beside me in the car, still shaking. Dahlia had offered her tea or brandy, but Evie had refused, so Marco had decided to take the even-more-distressed Dahlia back to her house.

I wrapped an arm around Evie's shoulders. "Red will be back soon. He just has to give his statement. Then he'll take you straight back to the Fentons' place."

"Th-thank you," Evie said. "I don't know why I'm still blubbering like a fool. I'm finally free of that nightmare. There were so many witnesses who saw how he threatened my life, he'll never survive in court this time. Thank goodness for your chauffeur."

Red opened the door and slid into the driver's seat. He placed the key in the ignition like it was just another day at work.

"That was amazing, Red," I said.

The chauffeur-bodyguard gave me a rueful look in the mirror. "I meant to take him out," he said.

"It was probably best that you didn't. You might have lost your job," I said. "As it is, I won't tell either of the Stones about this, if you don't."

Red nodded and hit the gas. When we arrived at the Fentons, I walked Evie up to the door and briefly explained her harrowing showdown to Ava. I deliberately omitted my own personal traumas of the day, knowing we could talk about that later.

Ava immediately went into comforting mother-figure mode, so I left knowing Evie was in the best of hands.

Red whisked me back to the Carrington estate. My stone cottage had never looked so inviting. Susan was sitting on the front step, two small bowls stacked beside her.

When Red opened the car doors, she rushed over and hugged first Red, then me. She focused on me. "Good heavens. Red texted something about how you were nearly killed, or maybe he was saying he nearly killed someone. I wasn't sure what he was talking about, so I brought two bowls of today's lobster bisque, one for each of you."

Red smiled—a wide smile of weary relief and happiness. He gave Susan a peck on the cheek. "That sounds just right."

As I trudged to my front door, Susan grabbed one of the bowls and handed it to me. "Do you want me to come in and fix you some herbal tea, honey? Maybe get you all snug with a blanket?"

Although the sun was shining, I was suddenly aware of the chill bumps on my arms. I wrapped my hands tighter around the warm bowl. "I'll be okay on my own," I said. "I just need to wind down. I'm sure I'll feel much better tomorrow. Thanks so much for dropping by and for the bisque."

She arched an eyebrow. "Are you sure, or are you just saying that to try to be polite?"

I managed a half smile. "I promise—I just need some time to myself. But I really appreciate both of you being there for me today. I can't even tell you how much." Feeling a burst of gratitude, I walked over to give Red a huge hug.

Susan, too, gave me a parting hug before I returned to my door. "Okay, well, you'd better call one of us if you need anything, okay? We'll be here lickety-split."

"Thank you."

Susan grabbed the second bowl of soup, then she linked arms with Red and he walked her to her car.

Once I had closed the door behind me, I glanced over the comforting sights of home: my favorite red Indian rug, my Chinese jade mementos, and my bookshelf overflowing with mysteries. My gaze landed on the small pot of pink poppies Jonas had brought me. As I stared at a bud that was about to open, I felt more than a twinge of homesickness for Larches Corner.

I pulled off my boots and flopped onto the couch, trying to process the fact that this could very well have been my last day on earth. I felt a pang, knowing how devastated my parents and my sister would have been, but I realized that Jonas and his mother would have truly mourned me, as well.

Stone the fifth was anyone's guess.

In what must have been a delayed response, my eyes filled and sobs shook my body. I grabbed a tissue and let myself wail until I felt cleansed.

Once I'd stopped my sniffling, I picked up my phone to call the people who'd been worried about me. They needed to know I was safe.

Realizing I had never called Veronica to let her know the wolf preserve murderer had been caught, and knowing that both Dahlia and Evie were probably too torn up to do it, I dialed her number first.

To say she was astonished when I described my cave encounter with Carson was an understatement.

"You mean Carson didn't even *like* me?" she asked, her nose stuffy. "It was all an act? But he was so…simpering, you know? So obsessed, I thought."

"According to my psychologist sister, psychopaths are great actors," I explained. "We were all fooled, especially since he was audacious enough to let the wolves chew on his own hand in order to throw suspicion off himself."

"That's messed up." She gave several hacking coughs. "Well, this just throws my thesis off-kilter. Now I'm going to have to go at the question another way."

Secretly, I was glad the wolves had been exonerated. "So, would you say the wolves look at humans as part of the pack, not as prey?"

"Yes, I'd definitely say that. Although they did chew on people—but that would seem pretty normal if they literally smelled like fresh meat. It's just so twisted to think of Carson rubbing meat on Shaun and Rich…"

"I know. You just can't let yourself go there." I hadn't even told Veronica about the showdown with Evie's ex. I figured Evie could tell her that part herself—*if* Evie and Veronica returned to work—and I didn't feel like rehashing it. "Do you think you're going to stick around a little longer at the preserve?" I asked hopefully.

The phone line was silent for a moment, then Veronica answered. "Yes. I believe I will. I feel horrible that I was going to be so slanted in my conclusions, making the wolves out to be ruthless killers." Her voice took on a fresh resolve. "I'll definitely hang around, at least until I get my thesis finished."

As I hung up with Veronica and called my parents, I made a snap decision. I would head home early for Easter. I needed time alone in the fields and woods, time to fish and ride the four-wheeler, and time to visit with Naomi Hawthorne.

* * * *

On Thursday, Detective Watson dropped by just as I was lugging my suitcase out the door. He took it from me and placed it in Bluebell's open trunk.

"Got yourself in a tight spot, I reckon," he said, his West Virginia accent strong. "After listening to Carson White's rambling statement, in which he mentioned you no fewer than ten times, I thought I'd drop by and check on you. He's not your everyday killer—more like the type that can get into your head—and I hoped he didn't get to you."

I thought of Carson's chilling screensaver message on my phone, which I'd since replaced with a picture of the soothing blue mountains of Dali in China. Just looking at the area in the Yunnan Province brought back wonderful memories of a day trip a friend and I had made there during my Peace Corps days. "I try not to think about him. But I am heading home for Easter, just to take a break from pet-sitting and Greenwich."

Detective Watson ran a hand through his cropped, graying hair. "Good idea. After sitting snakes and wolves, maybe you ought to look into a different line of work." He gave me a thoughtful look. "Hey, did you ever think of training to be a police detective?"

My mouth fell open. "Are you serious?"

He smiled. "Of course I am. You've helped us apprehend two murderers. Now, maybe you tend to show up at right place at the right time...or maybe you're seeing some things I'm missing."

"Or maybe I just attract weirdos," I said.

He chuckled. "I suppose that's a possibility, too. But I just wanted to give you something to think about. It's not easy—you have to work your way up—but if you ever think it's something you want to pursue, just let me know and we'll get the ball rolling."

He shook my hand and strode back to his car. I stood speechless, unable to think what I needed to do next.

Belinda Blake, police detective?

It did have a certain ring to it.

26

Jonas and I sat in a nook at The Coffee Shoppe, waiting for the other book clubbers of Larches Corner to arrive. He'd asked me to meet him early, so we could catch up.

"A detective?" he repeated, taking a sip of his house brew. "Is that something you really want to do?"

"I don't know. I've been thinking about it. I mean, why *do* I keep stumbling into these murderers? I think it's because I can't stop until I figure out what's going on. It seems like it would be a good fit for me—a *real* career, you know? But at the same time, I'm looking at four or five years of training and on-the-job experience. Katrina thinks I wouldn't want to stick it out, and she does know me well. I don't like feeling trapped in a job."

"I wonder why that is." He shot me an amused look.

"What're you saying, Jonas Hawthorne?" My tone was sharp.

He dropped his eyes, poking at the petals of a hot pink gerbera daisy that sat in a squatty vase on our table. "Just that, well, you know. I mean, your mom—"

I bristled. "You're saying I'm like my mom?"

He looked bewildered. "Why, is that a bad thing? Your mom's fantastic. She knows how to do just about anything."

I took a liberal drink of my strawberry frappe, mulling over his observation.

And I realized he was dead right. How had I not seen it all these years?

Although I'd always related most to my even-keeled dad, I couldn't escape the fact that I tended to hurtle from one idea to the next, trying first one thing, then another. And why? Because I was hoping to settle on something? No. It was because I got bored. I needed to have projects and live fully in the moment, just like my mom did.

Almost in slow motion, Jonas reached across the table and wrapped my hand in his own. It was the first time he'd made that kind of very intentional physical contact, and my hand warmed so quickly, it could've peeled the varnish off the table. He gave me an intense look. "Belinda, you never cease to surprise me. You're so different from—well, from anyone else I know. You're a delight."

It sounded like something my grandma would say, but when Jonas said it, a tingle ran through me. Especially when he was holding on to my hand like he didn't want to let go of it.

His voice deepened, and he leaned closer, his knee resting against mine under the table. "As a matter of fact, I've been wanting to talk with you—"

The bell jingled on the door, and Delia Jensen walked in. She was the only Female of Marriageable Age in the book club, and she looked like she could have been the muse for any number of beautiful Renaissance paintings. Her dark eyes flicked our way, and she lit up with a smile.

"Jonas." She turned from him to me. "And Belinda, lovely to see you're in town! I'll grab my coffee and come right over. I'm so looking forward to discussing Gatsby."

I tried to control the irrational jealousy that always flared when I saw Delia. I didn't think Jonas was enamored with her—in fact, he seemed rather taken with me at the moment—but I couldn't be sure.

To my dismay, he let go of my hand. "We'll talk soon," he promised.

As the rest of the book club trickled in, I tried to get my head back in the game. We discussed the role of truth and lies in *The Great Gatsby*, Nick's frequent inebriation throughout the book, and whether Daisy and Gatsby would have had as much appeal without their fortunes.

I glanced at Jonas. His face was twisted in distaste as he responded to the group leader's commendation of Tom Buchanan. Of course Jonas would have no time for Tom. Tom Buchanan was the type of louse I was pretty sure Jonas would beat up in real life.

Jonas was such a multidimensional man. A farmer who was always open to trying new methods of doing things. A caretaker who sacrificed his time and looked out for others without question. A student whose mind could never be satiated.

I wanted to hold his hand again.

* * * *

When we got to the truck, Jonas's mom called and asked if he could pick up some Sprite on the way home.

"She must be feeling sick again. It's the only thing she'll drink when she's sick," he said, his grip tight on the wheel.

We ran into the tiny convenience store in town for the Sprite. Usually when we wound up at this particular store together, we'd start reminiscing over how the old Coke machine would give free drinks if you pounded on it just right, or how the owner used to stock the favorite candy bars of each kid in the neighborhood. But today we shopped in silence. On the way home, Jonas could barely string three words together. This was no time to question him about the conversation he'd promised me.

When we reached my parents' white house, Mom came out to the truck and gave Jonas a warm greeting. Jonas didn't talk long, and as soon as I stepped out of the truck, he took off.

I tried to explain his abrupt behavior. "His mom's sick."

Mom grimaced. "I feel so bad for her. She's so young for all this." She dusted her dirty work gloves together. "Say, would you have a minute to come out back and help me set something up?"

"You mean your windmill? You're already working on that? But Tyler and Katrina just got in this morning."

"Wind *turbine*," Mom corrected me. "And Katrina's been snappish today, so Tyler's anxious to get outside."

Snappish was probably an understatement. Katrina was not a good patient, and being placed on bed rest had probably been demoralizing for her.

"Sure. I'll just run in to change and check in with Kat, and then I'll come out."

Mom's long blonde curls were twisted into a bun, and her face was sprinkled with quite a few more freckles than my own. My eyes traveled from her gloved hands to her flare-leg jeans, then finally to her scuffed boots that had weathered a lot of snow and rain. I felt a wave of gratefulness. I used to think Mom was fickle and unappeasable. Now I saw that she was determined, hopeful, and brave. She pushed to do hard things, and she never ran into a situation she didn't try to tackle head-on.

In fact, if I turned out exactly like her, I would stand proud. I pulled Mom into a tight hug.

She laughed. "What brought this on? Are you trying to get out of helping me?"

"Nope—I wouldn't dream of it. I'm just happy you're my mom."

She beamed. "And I'm thankful you're my daughter, Belinda Jade." She yanked a hat onto her head. "Now, let's get cracking."

* * * *

I grabbed a couple of Katrina's homemade cinnamon rolls before heading up to meet her. I found her curled up on the guest bed, her oversized stomach resting on a body pillow. She was watching a rerun of *Dr. Phil*, which by extension meant that she was shouting at the poor people who were unburdening their hearts on-screen.

"I can't believe you would say that to your wife," she said, gesturing wildly at the TV. "Your *wife*!"

I had no idea what the man had just said, but I knew it wasn't important. The real issue at hand was that Katrina was attempting to cope with her powerless state by bossing around people on TV.

I'd picked up a few psychological skills myself.

"Sis," I started, handing her a cinnamon roll, "I need to talk."

This was always a surefire way to calm Katrina down. There was nothing she liked better than to have a deep, soul-sharing discussion with someone.

"What's up?" she asked, taking a huge bite of the roll. She was definitely eating for two.

"Jonas wanted to talk with me about something, and it seemed important, but he wasn't able to work his way back around to it. He had to get home to his mom because she was sick."

She struggled to sit up. "You think he was going to ask you something more personal? I mean, he did bring you that refurbished bike, and he went to visit you in Greenwich...you never know. Are you hopeful he's going to get serious?"

"I don't know. He's...different...from the other guys I've dated."

She snorted. "You mean he's not a jerk."

"Yeah, I guess so. But then there's Stone—"

"You've described him so vividly." Katrina's voice was a bit swoony. "It's like he's a modern-day Gatsby, throwing those billiards parties and hobnobbing with all his rich, disaffected friends."

I hadn't even made the connection with Gatsby before, but Katrina had a point. And I wondered—would Stone Carrington the fifth hold the same appeal if he didn't have his fortune? If he wasn't such a little boy lost, the only child of wealthy parents who didn't have time for him?

Although he never flaunted his money, I had to admit that part of Stone's appeal was that he fit so perfectly into the shiny, opulent life that Greenwich represented. The bottom line was that I simply couldn't picture the man anywhere else.

And yet at this very moment, he was probably wearing burlap clothing and chanting mantras in Bhutan.

However, to be fair, normal people couldn't afford to jet off to Bhutan for an extended yoga retreat any old time they wanted. Even dressed in burlap, Stone couldn't escape his wealth.

Katrina's eyes fixed on me. Dietrich had once artistically described Katrina's eyes as "foggy green," which was quite accurate. He'd also said my eyes were a "bronze-dusted deep green." I had since conjectured that if he were painting them, they'd probably turn out some awful shade of bile.

"What's going on in that chaotic head of yours?" she asked.

I fell back into the bed. "Besides thinking about eye color, I don't know. I suppose I was comparing Stone and Jonas. Is that bad?"

"Perfectly normal," she said.

I waited for her to elaborate and tell me what to look for in a good man, but she didn't. I hoped things were going okay between her and Tyler—we all loved Tyler—but I decided not to pry. Most likely, her hormones were a little out of control at this stage of pregnancy.

"Could you scratch my back there?" she asked abruptly, pointing to an area near her spine.

"Sure."

As I started scratching, she seemed to relax. "So, do you want to talk about that freak who tried to kill you?"

The repetitive scratching movement was somehow therapeutic for me, too. "Carson. His name is Carson White."

My voice cracked as I said his last name. Apparently, I wasn't ready to unpack his thwarted murder attempt just yet.

Katrina twisted around and took my hand, her eyes fierce. "I wish I could've been there for you."

I knew that *if* my sister had been there, she would have figured out a way to kill Carson with her own two hands before the cops ever had a chance to reach us. Katrina was not the kind of woman to be trifled with, and she was like a roaring mother lion with those she loved.

"Thanks, sis. I do, too. Come and visit me in Greenwich sometime, okay?"

"I plan to, as soon as things settle down after Jasper's birth. Do you think you'll keep up your pet-sitting?"

I knew I'd have to get back into pet-sitting, but I'd decided to take a little break first. "I will, but I'm going to work on getting a Twitch stream going for my gaming—it's like a video channel."

She stretched and yawned. "Sounds like just the kind of thing you can throw yourself into—safely. Go for it."

Tyler came in, bearing another cinnamon roll for Katrina. "Great minds think alike," I said, standing. "Is Mom still working on the windmill? She's probably wondering what happened to me."

"It came together faster than we thought it would," Tyler said. He brushed his strawberry-blond bangs out of his eyes, and I thought again what a lovely contrast he made with Katrina, who was pale and dark-haired, like Vivien Leigh. "She might need a little help with the cleanup," he added, allowing his gaze to fall on Katrina's face. His look went from casual to PG-13 plus in a split second.

"I'll head out there now," I said, rushing out the door. As I pulled my boots on, I wondered, just for a moment, how nice it would be to have someone around who worshiped me the way Tyler seemed to worship Katrina. But then again, was that even the kind of guy I needed?

* * * *

Church on Easter Sunday was relaxing, even though quite a few of Mom's friends asked me pointedly if I was dating yet. Most of the aforementioned friends had bachelor sons, so I was cagey in my answers, insinuating there was someone I was interested in.

After a ham dinner, Tyler and Katrina bid us farewell and headed back to Albany. Dad had an emergency house call and Mom was tired, so I headed out on the four-wheeler for some fresh air. Without thinking, I drove straight through the fields toward Jonas's house.

I could see that he'd added to his beehives that ran along the woods. He was the kind of farmer who was always trying out unique new sources of revenue, selling everything from pumpkins to Christmas trees in season. I whisked along the outskirts of his yard, assuming he was either in the house or out milking cows at this time of day. I was wheeling around to return to my parents' when I saw him jogging toward me.

I geared down and stopped. "Hey there—happy Easter! Would it be okay if I came over tomorrow to see your mom?"

He shook his head, and my stomach dropped. "I only wish you could. She was admitted to the hospital today. I just ran home to grab some of her things. Her white cell count has dropped."

"Do you want me to go back with you?" I asked.

"No need. As it turns out, my brother is on his way home from Alaska— he'd planned to surprise us for Easter."

So the wandering Levi had made his way home. I hoped he would be a moral support to Jonas and his mom.

Jonas dropped his hand on my shoulder and his fingers inched toward my collarbone, jolting me out of my musings. "Belinda, I really do want to talk with you. I know you're heading back tomorrow, but promise you'll call me when you get to Greenwich."

"Okay." I hated being so helpless to ease his pain. "Anything you need, just call my parents' house, okay? Also, do you still leave your back door unlocked? I'll drop some ham off tonight for you and Levi—we have tons of leftovers."

"Yes, I'll leave it unlocked. Thanks, Belinda."

I gave him a brief, awkward hug, then climbed back on my four-wheeler and headed for the field. I flew through the tall grass, tears nearly blinding me. What I wouldn't give to be able to catch the most resistant and deadly killer of all—cancer.

27

Bluebell was a little wheezy as I pulled up to the carriage house, and I hoped I wouldn't have to take her in for more repairs. Once I'd paid my April rent and utilities, the money I'd earned at the White Pine Wolf Preserve wasn't going to stretch as far as I had hoped.

Val greeted me at the security booth. "Did you have a good trip?"

"I did," I said, noting the huge smile wreathed across his face. "What's new?"

"Nothing," he said, his smile stretching wider.

"You're obviously hiding something," I said.

He turned away from me, adjusting the computer screen in front of him. "I'm just glad to see you're back," he said.

"Yeah...right," I said, slowly pulling into the open gate. Something was up.

It took only one glance at the manor house to figure it out. Stone's yellow Lamborghini sat parked right outside the front door.

Was Red taking it out for a spin? Given Val's weird behavior, that didn't seem the most likely explanation.

I parked Bluebell in my driveway, grabbed some custom-roasted coffee I'd brought back from The Coffee Shoppe, and stepped onto the Carringtons' front lawn. My plan was to offer the coffee as an Easter gift, then sniff around a bit to see if Stone the fifth was back.

As I reached the halfway point, I saw a tall man with longer, dark hair emerging from the house. Stone the fourth wasn't that tall, and his dark hair wasn't that long.

It had to be Stone the fifth, back from Bhutan.

As if sensing my presence, he glanced my way, then gave me a vigorous wave. He tossed a couple of tennis rackets into his passenger seat and ran over to meet me.

He flung his arms wide for a hug. "Belinda! You're back! Val told me you were up at your parents' for Easter."

I walked into his arms, immediately overwhelmed by the proximity of his masculine scent. "I just got home." I pulled back, examining his stubble beard and longer locks. He was even tanner than usual, and when he pushed his sunglasses up on his head, his eyes crinkled around the edges.

He looked healthier than I'd ever seen him.

"The yoga retreat was good for you," I observed.

He laughed. "Actually, I left the retreat before the second week was over. I couldn't handle the vegetarian food, and I couldn't do half the poses anyway. I checked into a hotel and ordered myself a steak to clear my head. Then I decided I'd concoct my own regimen, which included a personal trainer every morning and a masseuse every night. During the days, I trekked up mountains or swam in the outdoor pool. And I didn't do a lick of work."

He extended an arm and flexed, revealing a honed bicep. "Check it out! Impressive, isn't it? I've never been so ripped before. Wait till Dietrich sees me!"

I couldn't hold back my laugh. Stone was as giddy as a teenage boy. And goofy, too. "So you paid all that money for a retreat you didn't even attend?" I asked.

"They gave me my money back," he said. He focused his stunning aqua eyes on me. "You should travel with me sometime. We'd have a blast. Have you ever gone paragliding?"

"I haven't." It sounded fun, but right now, I was in the mood to retreat from danger, rather than charge into it.

He studied my face. "That was thoughtless of me. I've been going on and on about myself, but I know you've had an eventful time right here in Greenwich. Red told me a few things about your wolf-sitting venture, but he didn't go into detail. I feel like we need to catch up."

I felt tired, unable to describe the horrors I'd experienced at White Pine. And I needed to think my story through, so I didn't spill the beans about Red's near-fatal protective shooting incident. "Why don't you come over tomorrow night and we'll talk," I said. "I can make dinner."

Stone shook his head. "I won't hear of it. You just got back. Lani will be happy to make something special for us."

Lani was the Carringtons' sweet Hawaiian cook, and she loved nothing more than to dote on Stone the fifth, since she'd been with the Carringtons since Stone was just a tyke.

"That would be wonderful," I said, looking at his Lamborghini. "So, what are you up to today? Tennis?"

He nodded. "Would you believe the police are finally removing the Breathalyzer device from my car? So now I won't feel like an idiot driving around town. Once I'm free of that thing, I'm going to hit the courts with some buddies of mine."

I was thrilled at the progress Stone had made. "Stone, I know you kicked your alcoholism last year, but how's your dad doing with his? He wasn't around much while you were gone."

"He's doing fine, as far as I know. Lani said he asked her to sweep the house for liquor and dump it all down the drain—even his prized Rémy Martin cognac."

"I'm so glad to hear that."

Stone glanced at his car. "I'd better get going. But see you tomorrow night?"

"Yes, why don't you come around seven—and be sure to bring the food." I grinned.

He swept into a bow. "'Twill be my pleasure to do so, m'lady."

* * * *

Veronica called me the next morning, wondering if I could help her set up a website. "I'm going to blog about the wolves at White Pine," she said. "Kind of as a penance, you know? There I was, ready to throw them under the bus for the murders, but they were just as much victims as you were."

When I asked how Dahlia was, Veronica didn't give me a straight answer. "Evie's been doing a lot to manage things right now," she said. "She's been really happy lately, chatting with her parents about her move back to Britain. And Marco's come in every day. His nephew Antonio is helping out, too, and I think they might hire him full-time."

"And Carson?" I couldn't stop myself from asking.

"Lawyered-up, as you'd imagine," she grumbled. "But Jacob says they have some DNA evidence on him, so I doubt he'll be able to get off scot-free."

I was pretty certain Veronica wasn't supposed to share that information with me, but I was pleased she had.

We agreed to meet the next day at the library so I could help set up her site. As I hung up, I was thankful that it sounded like the White Pine Wolf Preserve would go on, even with Dahlia limping along at the helm.

* * * *

Stone showed up early. He was fresh-shaven and had gotten a haircut, which served to highlight his angled cheekbones. He looked about as Greenwich as they came, wearing a blue-checked poplin shirt and white pants. I felt underdressed in my jeans and my red blouse, but Stone couldn't seem to look away from me, so I guessed I'd chosen the right outfit for the evening.

We laid out the food from Lani, both of us exclaiming over the variety of it. She'd included a radish and corn salad, flank steak with shallot mustard sauce, homemade fries, and individual salted caramel chocolate tarts.

"It's like she knows both of us so well," I said.

He set another plate on the table. "She prides herself in reading people quickly—figuring out their food likes and dislikes."

"Which explains why she made steak—she knew you weren't about to go vegetarian." I laughed.

As we sat down with our salad, Stone got serious. "Listen, while I was in Bhutan, I did manage to do what I'd hoped to, which was to evaluate the direction my life was heading."

I chewed in silence, giving him a reassuring nod.

"The thing is…I've only had one relationship in my life that's felt really stable and encouraging. And that relationship is with you, Belinda."

I coughed, nearly choking on a piece of corn.

Relationship? He called this a relationship? We'd barely even dated.

"Are you serious?" I managed to ask.

He looked hurt. "Yes, definitely. I know it's not a clearly defined relationship—things basically went nuts before Christmas, but when I was with you, I had the most fun I've ever had. You're exciting and unpredictable, and…you make me happy. I found myself thinking about you every day I was gone—your curls, your gorgeous eyes, and—"

He slid his chair closer. His hand lowered onto the table, and his long fingers closed around mine. It was only when he leaned down, his eyes closed, that I realized he was going to kiss me.

I had initiated a kiss with Stone once, on the beach, and that time it was like something had basically possessed my senses and drawn me to him like a magnet. But at this moment, I found myself pulling back, my free hand shooting toward his chest to stop him.

He blinked and froze, as if he'd been smacked. His hopeful eyes searched mine, waiting.

He was waiting for an answer I couldn't give him.

My heart was tangled up with someone else. I couldn't extricate my mind from what Jonas was doing right now—probably sitting by his mother's hospital bedside, or maybe picking his brother up from the airport.

"I...can't," I said.

Stone's jaw flexed. "It's okay." He let go of my hand. "Really, it's totally okay."

"But you don't understand—" I began.

He jumped to his feet. "Let's eat our dessert and pretend this didn't happen, okay?"

When he said that, I knew. Just like Daisy Buchanan, I'd made my choice, and I didn't think Stone would be anywhere near as loyal and unrelenting as Gatsby was.

I'd barely escaped being murdered by a psychopath, but now I felt like I had stepped into the middle of my own perfect storm.

What was a girl to do?

Printed in the United States
by Baker & Taylor Publisher Services